PAGES AND PREMONITIONS

A SPELLBOUND BOOKSHOP PARANORMAL COZY MYSTERY

BOOK 1

J. A. WHITING

Copyright 2024 J.A. Whiting and Whitemark Publishing

Cover copyright 2024 Signifer Book Design

Formatting by Signifer Book Design

Proofreading by Donna Rich (donnarich@me.com) and Riann Kohrs (www.riannkohrs.com)

This book is a work of fiction. Names, characters, places, or incidents are products of the author's imagination or are used fictitiously. Any resemblance to locales, actual events, or persons, living or dead, is entirely coincidental.

All rights reserved.

No part of this publication can be reproduced or transmitted in any form or by any means, electronic or mechanical, without permission in writing from J. A. Whiting.

To hear about new books and book sales, please sign up for my mailing list at:
jawhiting.com

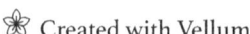 Created with Vellum

Use your magic for good

1

The scent of freshly baked blueberry muffins wafted through the apartment above the cozy bookshop as Shelby Price hurried to get ready for the start of her workday. As the owner and proprietor of Spellbound Books in the charming New England town of Hamlet, Massachusetts, Shelby always liked to have warm treats waiting for her customers when she unlocked the front door at 8:00 am. She hummed to herself as she got dressed and brushed her long, brown hair, pausing to give her cat Harper an affectionate scratch behind the ears before heading downstairs with the tray of muffins.

The striped gray and white Maine Coon lazily stretched and followed the young woman down the staircase and into the shop, knowing that customers would be arriving soon and many of them would shower the cat with attention. Shelby smiled. Harper was as popular as some of the new bestsellers on display.

She tidied up the already neat and welcoming store, plumping pillows on the overstuffed chairs by the fireplace, arranging the muffins on the counter, and starting pots of coffee.

Spellbound Books occupied a prime location on Hamlet's picturesque Main Street surrounded by other local businesses like Bread and Roses Bakery, The Quilted Heart Fabric Shop, and Maggie's Candle Company. Shelby had dreamed of owning her own bookstore in her hometown since she was a little girl. After graduating from Boston University with a degree in literature and business, she had scrimped and saved every penny to make her dream a reality, and two years ago, at the age of twenty-five, she had done just that.

Owning a bookshop in the age of eBooks and online retail was a risky venture, but Shelby loved the tactile joy of print books and the serendipity of discoveries found browsing packed shelves. She focused on stocking a wide variety of titles from current fiction to cookbooks to children's stories and hosted interesting author events and book clubs.

Her gamble paid off - Spellbound Books now enjoyed a loyal, local customer base in addition to a steady stream of tourists attracted by the town's old-fashioned charm.

Originally called Salem's Sister City, Hamlet was founded in the late 1600s by Puritan settlers seeking religious freedom and fertile farmland. The town sat near the rocky New England coastline not far from the better-known tourist destination of Salem. Hamlet had its own rich history with spooky legends of ghosts, witches, and unexplained occurrences dating back centuries. The fascinating tales only added to the area's mystique and appeal to sightseers.

Shelby loved telling visitors about the most notorious Hamlet legend which involved the ghost of a tormented young woman named Prudence Harris. Prudence was born in Salem in 1676 and was nearly tried as a witch during the Witch Trials when she was only seventeen years old. She narrowly escaped the hangman's noose thanks to the efforts of her merchant father who arranged her secret exile to relatives living in the Virginia colony. Prudence fled south but never made it to Virginia, disappearing somewhere along the way.

According to local lore, Prudence's restless spirit

haunted the sprawling Harris Estate on the outskirts of town where her family had moved after leaving Salem, hopelessly searching for her lost home and relatives.

Shelby occasionally joined the crowds on nights when the historical society offered candlelight tours of the supposedly haunted grounds. She hadn't spotted any ghostly apparitions herself, but hearing the tragic tale of Prudence Harris always gave her a satisfying spook.

Shelby enjoyed the glances both backward and forward that living in Hamlet provided. Surrounded by the reminders of the past and its mysteries, she looked ahead to the promises the future held. She saw herself spending happy days living in the apartment over the bookshop, enjoying little pleasures like cooking with ingredients from the local farmer's market or curling up with a new book on a rainy evening.

As the clock struck eight, Shelby went to unlock the front door and flip over the "Closed" sign. Harper twined happily around the young woman's ankles, eager to assume her customary morning post greeting the customers.

"Ready for another day, Harper?" Shelby asked affectionately, and a loud meow came in response.

The cat took up her position by the checkout desk while Shelby busied herself straightening a display of the newest releases. She paused when she came across an advance copy of the latest thriller from one of her favorite authors. Tucking the novel under her arm to read later, Shelby glanced around the shop with a feeling of contentment. She loved seeing people browse the overflowing bookshelves searching for stories to get lost in, or to find new information to absorb. Owning Spellbound Books was Shelby's long-held dream. She couldn't imagine a better life.

The cheerful jangling of the bell over the door as the first customers arrived interrupted Shelby's thoughts. She straightened up with a welcoming smile on her face.

Harper hopped down and trotted over to investigate the new arrivals.

"Good morning. Let me know if I can help you find anything," Shelby called out. With a little sigh, she turned back to the new releases display. She always felt a little uneasy when approaching someone she didn't know, but over the past two years, she'd made good progress in becoming more comfortable chatting with new customers at the shop. She supposed her gentle shyness was an odd personality quirk for someone who owned a retail store.

Shelby went into the backroom and came out with a step ladder she set up in front of the fireplace. It was already the weekend after Thanksgiving and she still hadn't finished putting up Christmas decorations. After the Thanksgiving meal, Shelby and her relatives had made wreaths in the big red barn behind her parents' house, and hers was a huge evergreen wreath with red ribbons, shiny ornaments, and tiny white lights. Carrying it as she stepped up the ladder, she reached for the hammer she'd placed on the mantelpiece. Suddenly, the weight of the wreath caused her balance to shift and her foot slipped off the step.

With a cry of surprise, Shelby felt herself falling backwards. Tumbling off the ladder, she fell into a heap as her head cracked sharply on the floor. After losing consciousness for several seconds, her eyes popped open to find herself lying stunned on the hardwood floor.

The cat's face leaned over her, staring down at the young woman. "You hit your head, but you're fine," the cat told her. "You'll have a doozy of a headache though."

Shelby's face paled as she looked at Harper. *Are you talking to me?!*

"Yes, I am. Finally, you can hear me." Harper flicked her tail. "But don't worry, no one else can ... only you."

"Oh, my goodness! Are you all right?" An anxious female voice filtered through the daze clouding Shelby's brain. She felt gentle hands assisting her as she slowly sat up, gingerly touching the growing lump on the back of her head.

"I think so," Shelby said shakily. "What happened?"

The woman who had helped Shelby to her feet was tall and elegantly dressed, wearing an old-fashioned traveling coat and a hat with a spotted veil. She shook her head, blue eyes crinkling with concern under the hat's brim.

"You must have slipped," the woman said, her voice refined and vaguely British. "One second, you were up on the ladder, and the next, you were flat on the floor."

Shelby climbed unsteadily to her feet, the kind stranger assisting with a grip on her elbow. The throbbing ache in her head made it hard to focus, but Shelby didn't think she had a concussion or anything dire wrong with her. She glanced at Harper, giving the cat an odd look.

"I appreciate your help," she told the woman gratefully. "I'll have to be more careful from now on when I'm hanging decorations."

The elegant woman nodded sympathetically.

"No lasting harm done, I hope," she said. "Do take care." With a gentle pat on Shelby's shoulder, the woman turned and exited the shop.

Staring after her for a long moment, something niggled at the back of her mind. Shaking her head regretfully - and then wincing when the motion made the pain pound more fiercely - she headed for the employee break room and an ice pack.

Ten minutes later, the painful lump on the back of Shelby's head had changed to a dull throb. She figured she was lucky not to have more serious injuries from her slip and fall.

Shelby gave Harper a reassuring cuddle to calm her feline anxiety after witnessing the accident. "I thought you spoke to me right after I hit the floor. How crazy is that?"

Harper remained silent.

The regular morning crowd had picked up, and Shelby needed to get busy. Her friend and employee

Rachel would arrive just before lunch to help out for the rest of the day.

Soon she was busy helping customers find books and making cheerful small talk. The normal, busy work routine pushed uneasy thoughts about falling off the ladder and hearing her cat speak out of Shelby's mind. When Rachel burst through the front door right on time at 11:30 am in her perpetually rushed state, Shelby had nearly forgotten about her tumble.

"You look really nice today," Shelby said in greeting, noting the extra care Rachel had taken with styling her long, dark curls. "Big date tonight?" she kidded.

Rachel's pale cheeks turned crimson as she shifted the impressive stack of books she lugged in her arms. At twenty-seven, the same age as Shelby, Rachel still hadn't outgrown the tendency to blush at the slightest provocation. Shelby hid a smile, deciding not to tease her easily flustered friend any further.

"Just drinks after work with Chad from the coffee shop," Rachel mumbled, keeping her gaze fixed on the books she was unpacking. "No big deal."

Shelby had suspected for a while that Rachel's constant trips to Bread and Roses Bakery next door had more to do with chatting with the cute barista than a desire for muffins or scones. She hoped caffeine wouldn't be the only thing brewing between her friend and Chad. They would make such a cute couple.

Harper sauntered over to inspect the new shipment of cat-themed notebooks Rachel was stocking on a shelf. After giving them an approving sniff, she wandered back to the front windowsill where she sat surveying the foot traffic outside.

Shelby smiled knowing the capricious cat's loyalty could be bought with the right treats or chin scratches.

The rest of the morning passed quickly between assisting customers and keeping up with restocking inventory. Shelby spent her lunch break in the back room devouring one of the new thriller novels, too caught up in the twists and turns of the mystery plot to return to the front of the store until Rachel poked her head in and asked if she was coming back out onto the floor.

"Oh, sorry. Time got away from me." Shelby reluctantly tucked the thriller under the counter to grab again on her way upstairs when the work day was over. Reading was usually how she relaxed after work, often staying up far too late to find out what happened next in whatever book had captured her imagination.

A few minutes after flipping the sign to "Closed" at 6:00 pm, Shelby ushered the last customer out with a cheery goodbye. Rachel hurried to start the closing tasks of restocking shelves and tidying displays, clearly in a rush to leave for her date.

Shelby didn't mind doing the inventory and counting the till on her own. "Why don't you head out? You and Chad have fun." Shelby didn't have to tell Rachel twice to finish her shift. The young woman whirled out the front door in a flutter of silky scarves and flowy skirt.

Shaking her head in amusement, Shelby headed to the backroom to finish up the end-of-day routine. She promised herself plenty of time that night to sit and read her new book, ignoring the tiny pinch of loneliness she sometimes felt at having no exciting evening plans with a boyfriend of her own.

An unexpected noise coming from the front of the store interrupted Shelby's closing work. She crept toward the doorway connecting the back area to the main bookshop, grabbing a hefty hardcover murder mystery as an improvised weapon ... just in case.

Maybe Rachel forgot something after leaving? she wondered.

"Hello? We're closed," Shelby announced as she stepped back onto the sales floor.

There was no response. Feeling uneasy, she looked all around but saw no signs of an intruder, and then scolded herself for letting her imagination run wild. Working in a building rumored to be haunted sometimes made her a little jumpy. With a wry chuckle, Shelby replaced the weighty hardcover on a display table. Time to finish closing up and head upstairs.

A soft thump sounded again from the direction of the front counter, making Shelby yelp in fright. This was no product of her overactive imagination - something had just knocked a book off a shelf just out of her sight. For a split-second, Shelby considered making a run for the exit but shook off the foolish feeling. She grabbed the heavy book again for self-defense and inched forward.

"I'm calling the police if someone is messing around in here," Shelby threatened, trying to keep the quaver out of her voice. She inched closer to the front area, prepared to confront either a confused customer who had accidentally been left behind or a brazen shoplifter.

Shelby halted in shock when she reached the checkout counter. A book was levitating in mid-air, its pages fluttering as if an invisible person were browsing through them. She watched open-mouthed as the novel settled back on the countertop, only to have another float up right after it. Shelby stared, unable to process what she was witnessing.

Before she could recover her wits enough to run for help, Shelby felt a cold tingling sensation envelop her body. Her muscles tensed against the chilling pressure surrounding her. Panic flooded her veins as darkness seeped into the edges of Shelby's vision and the room began to fade away. Fighting against the blackness, she struggled to stay conscious.

In desperation, she clutched the back of a chair, not wanting to fall down again, and took slow, deep breaths. As Shelby forced herself to focus every ounce of energy into remaining calm, she lifted one hand to her throat where the rose quartz pendant she always wore lay against her frigid skin.

Trying to slow down her racing heart, the biting cold left as quickly as it had arrived. She stumbled forward and grabbed onto the solid wood of the checkout counter desk, anchoring herself against it.

She stood there for endless minutes, waiting for her tingling numbness to fade and rational thought to return.

What she had just seen wasn't a natural occurrence. She wasn't prone to flights of fancy, but living in Hamlet she did believe in the paranormal – although nothing like that had ever happened to her before.

The only explanation her logical mind could accept was that a ghost or spirit of some sort had been in her bookstore. Shelby reached for her pendant.

Raising a still-shaky hand to the tender lump on her head, Shelby wondered if getting knocked out earlier had jostled something loose in her brain.

She shook herself. She must have imagined the bizarre incident. Ghostly books lifting off shelves by themselves and hearing her cat speak to her had to be delusions brought on by hitting her head.

Right?

Shelby couldn't accept she had a phantom in her shop reading her books. What would she tell the police - that an invisible assailant had been picking out books? They would cart her straight to the psych ward.

Leaning against the counter for a few long

moments trying to calm herself, she tried to decide what course of action to take. She jumped when a soft furry shape brushed against her leg. Looking down into the bemused green eyes of her cat, Shelby exhaled a shaky laugh. She gave the feline a gentle scratch under her chin.

"You wouldn't know what just happened here, would you, sweet one?" she asked the cat.

Harper purred and leaned harder into the young woman's hand, unbothered by supernatural manifestations.

"Just keep scratching." Shelby heard the cat's words in her head.

"What?" Shelby stepped back from her fluffy cat. "Did you say something?"

"Yes, Shelby, I did."

"Maybe I should call the doctor." With a deep breath, Shelby rubbed her head trying to pull herself together. She had to get out of there - she could figure out an explanation for what she'd experienced later. Right then, all she wanted was to be safely locked in her cozy apartment with all the lights blazing.

Gathering her things in a hurry, the young woman dashed up the interior stairs hidden behind the store's stockroom with Harper following her, for once not bothering to be sure she'd shut off the lights in the bookshop. She locked the apartment door behind them and went around turning on every light.

Collapsing onto her overstuffed couch, Shelby tried to slow her still panicked breathing. She couldn't stop replaying the bizarre and terrifying incidents over and over in her mind, analyzing every detail of the unbelievable experiences.

Had her cat spoken to her?

Had she really seen a book floating in midair, lifted from the counter by an invisible hand?

No, it wasn't possible. She fumbled for explanations. She must have knocked her head harder than she realized that morning, resulting in the vivid hallucinations. That had to be the only plausible solution.

But despite her best efforts, Shelby couldn't banish the lingering uneasy feeling that she hadn't imagined any of it. Something strange had happened in the bookshop after she'd fallen off the ladder. She didn't know what that something was - but she intended to find out.

Shelby looked down at Harper, now snoozing on her lap as if nothing was amiss. "What do you say, should we do some investigating?" she murmured.

The only response was a flick of a gray ear.

Trying to ignore her fear, Shelby picked up the new novel she had placed on the coffee table when she'd come home. She stared blankly at the pages without comprehending the words, too distracted by racing thoughts to focus on the story. Sighing in defeat, she set the book aside.

She had a mystery of her own to occupy her thoughts.

2

After dozing off for a few minutes on the comfortable sofa in her cozy living room, Shelby woke with a start, her head still reeling from the bizarre events that had happened at the bookshop. She couldn't erase the image of a novel hovering in mid-air or the sound of Harper's voice speaking words only she seemed able to hear.

"I must have hit my head a lot harder than I thought," Shelby muttered, absently stroking the cat snuggled on her lap. Harper lifted her head, fixing her intelligent green eyes on Shelby's worried face.

"You're not losing your mind, Shelby. I really can speak to you now."

Shelby jerked in surprise, nearly toppling the

purring cat from her lap. "Did you just ... talk? Did you really just talk?" she asked incredulously.

Harper flicked an ear, looking faintly amused. "Of course. We have a lot to discuss now that you're able to hear me."

"This isn't possible," Shelby objected faintly, even as her mind raced to comprehend the implication of carrying on a conversation with her formerly mute pet. "Cats can't talk."

Harper sat up regally, wrapping her plumed tail neatly around her paws and said, "Perhaps not under normal circumstances, but you suffered a blow to the head, which seems to have awakened your psychic ability that allows you to understand my speech."

Shelby carefully set the cat on the floor and stood up, pressing both hands to her still-tender head. "Psychic powers? You must be joking. I need to lie down. I think I have a concussion."

With a gentle nudge of her head against Shelby's leg, Harper directed the unsettled young woman back to the couch.

"Your mind is clear," the cat told her. "This is no concussion or hallucination. You were always sensitive, though you suppressed your intuition in favor of logic and reason. Your injury disrupted the barricades around your inner eye."

Shelby stared at the talking feline with a dozen arguments right on the tip of her tongue, but gazing into Harper's eyes, she felt her doubts fade. On some level, this all made sense. Shelby had experienced strong intuition and hunches her entire life, though she often dismissed them as imagination. Maybe her perception really had been enhanced somehow when she hit her head.

"Okay," Shelby said slowly. "Let's say I believe you, and this new ability to ... to read your mind is real. Why me? And what does it have to do with the strange things I saw in the bookshop tonight?"

Harper settled back down, tucking her paws underneath her. "You have a bright spirit that's receptive to sights and sounds beyond the ordinary. As for what happened after you closed the shop, I suspect someone from Hamlet's past was trying to make contact."

A shiver danced down Shelby's spine at the memory of the book floating in the air. "A ghost, you mean?"

"Yes," Harper replied. "There are many restless souls tied to this land. You may have the power to help lay their burdens to rest." The cat didn't want to say anything more, not wanting to overwhelm her owner.

Shelby leaned her head back against the soft cushions, her brow furrowed. She had never given serious consideration to Hamlet's haunted history and exciting tales of witches, ghosts, and magic. Some of her family members had written off the supernatural stories as fanciful legends meant to draw in tourists. Could there be some truth to the local lore after all?

The sound of footsteps mounting the exterior stairs to the second-floor porch outside her apartment door interrupted Shelby's swirling thoughts. She had nearly forgotten her standing movie night with her best friend Lucy Blake. Lucy, a pastry chef at a bed-and-breakfast inn in the center of town, gently knocked twice before bursting through the door, arms laden with her promised caramel popcorn and a bottle of wine.

"Hey, sorry I'm late. The caramel took longer to get to that perfect gooey stage. Hope you picked a good movie for us...."

Lucy's voice trailed off as she took in the sight of Shelby sitting motionless on the couch, her face pale and eyes wide. Her usually polished wavy hair was falling down around her face.

"Shelby, what's wrong? You look like you've seen a ghost." Lucy quickly set down her offerings and hurried to her friend's side.

Shaking herself, Shelby tried to summon a reassuring smile for her concerned friend. "I'm okay, really. I'm just a little rattled by something that happened at the shop earlier this morning. I fell off a ladder hanging up decorations and hit my head."

"Oh no! Are you all right?" Lucy peered anxiously into Shelby's eyes, checking her pupils, then ran gentle fingers over the large lump on the back of her scalp. "That's a nasty bump. You might have a concussion. You need to go to the doctor tomorrow."

Shelby captured Lucy's fluttering hands in her own and squeezed them. "I promise to get checked out if the pain gets any worse or if I start to feel confused. It's just a bump, though. I was only out for a couple of seconds."

Lucy still looked doubtful, but she finally nodded. "Okay, but I'm keeping an eye on you tonight to make sure you don't start vomiting or passing out on me. Concussions are nothing to mess around with."

Shelby smiled. Trust Lucy to fuss over her - she had been a nurturer and a worrier since they met as children.

Shelby let Lucy coax her to the kitchen island while she prepared mugs of chamomile tea with lavender honey from a local store. Soon they were curled up together under a blanket in front of the TV, Harper joining them to bask in the extra attention.

Sipping her tea slowly, Shelby listened as Lucy chattered about her day spent rearranging furniture in the rooms of the bed and breakfast where she worked. Besides her love of baking, Lucy also enjoyed styling and designing spaces and was never content to let the decor remain the same for long.

Shelby made agreeable noises while her own thoughts drifted. She still felt unsettled by her encounter with the supernatural force in the bookshop and the unbelievable fact that she could now hear her cat talk to her. Part of her wanted to confess the baffling events to level-headed Lucy, who would set things back to normal.

But another part of Shelby hesitated. She knew once she told Lucy there would be no taking it back or pretending it never happened. Saying the words out loud would make the strange incidents real in a way Shelby wasn't sure she could handle. Maybe some fears were better left unspoken.

Shelby nearly jumped out of her skin when she

felt Harper's soft paw touch her arm. The cat's luminous eyes bored into hers.

"Tell her, Shelby. Don't carry this alone. She'll understand."

Blowing out a long breath, Shelby set down her mug on the coffee table. "I need to tell you something. Something weird happened at the store after I hit my head. Promise you won't think I'm crazy?"

Lucy muted the television and shifted to face her friend, her brow furrowing in concern again. "Of course, I won't think you're crazy. Well, maybe a little crazy," she teased. "What's going on?"

Haltingly at first, and then with increasing urgency, Shelby described the floating book, the icy blast of unnatural cold, and the sense of a presence in the shop. Finally, she voiced the unbelievable claim that she now possessed the ability to communicate telepathically with her cat.

"I know it sounds insane," Shelby concluded helplessly. "I must have imagined it all after getting knocked out, right?"

She searched Lucy's face anxiously for reassurance, but her friend looked thoughtful rather than dismissive.

"Honestly, I don't think you made this up," Lucy said finally. She held up a hand when Shelby started to object. "Hear me out. We both know Hamlet has a long history of weird supernatural stuff happening, and you said yourself your head feels fine, no double vision or nausea. So maybe when you fell, it unlocked some psychic ability you already had."

Shelby just stared, dumbfounded, as Lucy continued in a matter-of-fact tone. "You always had great intuition. When we were kids, you'd get feelings about things that came true. You just wrote it off as coincidence, but what if you were sensing things all along?"

Lucy leaned forward; her blue eyes were full of interest. "Have you tried reading Harper's mind again since you got home? Let's test it. Here, I'll think of a number between one and twenty. You ask Harper to tell you what it is."

"Oh, come on," Shelby laughed uncertainly. "You don't really think I can read the cat's thoughts, do you?"

Lucy kept a serious expression on her face. "Just try it." She leaned toward the cat and whispered a number to her.

Too weak to argue, Shelby looked down at the watching cat. Feeling ridiculous, she silently asked Harper, "Can you tell me the number Lucy is thinking of?"

The cat glanced at Lucy and blinked slowly. "The number is seven."

Shelby's jaw dropped. She whirled to gape at her friend. "She said seven. Is that right?"

Looking equally stunned, Lucy muttered, "Holy crap, that's right. You heard Harper say the number to you? That's amazing. This is incredible."

The reality of what she'd done slammed into Shelby like a freight train. She really could understand Harper's thoughts. This had to be an injury-induced hallucination.

Shelby jumped up from the sofa. "I think I need some air." She grabbed a sweater and headed for the second-floor balcony connected to her apartment, ignoring Lucy's worried protests.

Outside, Shelby gripped the railing with white knuckles, gazing blindly at the town lights twinkling below as she struggled to accept this new and terrifying reality.

Harper's revelation was genuine - Shelby really did have psychic powers. She wasn't losing her mind, but it was expanding in unbelievable ways.

The balcony door creaked open behind her, and Lucy's arm slipped around Shelby's shoulders. "I know it's a lot to take in," she whispered, "but we'll figure it out. It will be okay."

Turning to her friend, Shelby's vision blurred with grateful tears. "I'm scared. I don't understand what's happening to me."

"Shh, it's okay." Lucy pulled Shelby into a hug. "This is big and weird, but we'll figure it out."

They stood that way for several long moments until the chilly night air drove them inside. Shelby curled back in her spot on the sofa, Harper in her lap, and Lucy's shoulder pressed warmly against hers. The familiar bonds steadied her churning emotions. She took a deep breath.

"So, where do I go from here? I can't ignore what's happening to me, but I don't know how to handle it."

Lucy bit her lip thoughtfully. "I think we know someone who can help. Let's go talk to Fiona. I think she's working tonight."

Sixty-five-year-old Fiona Medley owned a little witchy boutique on Main Street called Crow's Crossing, where she sold all sorts of witch-inspired clothing and accessories.

Shelby nodded. She had often admired the New Age shop's ethereal music, intriguing window displays, and merchandise, and Fiona was always pleasant and friendly when she'd visited the store.

"This town is full of people who believe in magic.

You couldn't be in a better place to find the help you need. Fiona is supposed to be a real practicing witch. She does readings and spells and stuff," Lucy continued. "I bet she could teach you more about your abilities and how to use them."

Shelby weighed the suggestion. Learning from an experienced witch or psychic or whatever Fiona was seemed like her best option. This wasn't something she could just look up on the internet, and Fiona was discreet - Shelby didn't want her sudden extrasensory powers broadcast all around town. She exhaled, feeling the rightness of the decision.

"Okay, let's talk with Fiona. Hopefully, she can provide some guidance."

Lucy beamed. "Don't worry," she said reassuringly. "It's going to be amazing once you learn about your abilities and train them."

Despite her nervousness, Shelby found Lucy's enthusiasm contagious. With her friend by her side and a mentor like Fiona to help navigate the uncharted waters, Shelby felt a glimmer of excitement breaking through her panic. A sixth sense was nothing to fear - she would learn about it and try to make it her own. If nothing else, it would be an adventure. She hoped.

She turned to the cat. "What do you think, Harper?"

Harper bumped her head affectionately against Shelby's hand, a contented purr rumbling deep inside her. "You'll be all right. I'll help you on your journey," the cat said to the young woman's mind, "and Lucy will help, too."

"Maybe I'm not losing my mind," Shelby whispered as she stroked the soft fur, feeling grateful for the unwavering support of her closest friend and her sweet cat. She had allies for whatever lay ahead. The future felt uncertain but no longer as daunting as it had a few hours ago, now that she had Lucy and Harper standing with her.

Shelby took comfort in the ancient words of wisdom, whispering reassuringly in her heart: *When the student is ready, the teacher will appear.*

3

Shelby stepped out into the bracing night air with Lucy at her side and Harper's warm weight cradled in her arms. Her world had shifted in a few short hours, leaving her reeling, but talking to the friendly witch Fiona might bring some much-needed answers.

"It sure is cold," Lucy said, linking her arm through Shelby's, "but the fresh air will do us both good."

As they set off up Main Street, Shelby admired the familiar storefronts decorated for the holidays with pine garlands, red bows, and white lights. The festive charm of her little town soothed some of her inner turmoil. Hamlet was home, a place of safety - surely nothing too alarming could happen here.

As they approached the pretty facade of Crow's Crossing, Shelby's nerves returned. The store was closed, but the windows still glowed from a few lights on inside. Shelby and Lucy could see Fiona moving about in the shop.

Fiona had always seemed perfectly ordinary on Shelby's few visits to the shop's candles, crystals, and hippie-chic clothes, but learning the friendly shopkeeper practiced witchcraft made her feel uneasy.

Shelby slowed, clutching Harper tighter. "Maybe this isn't a good idea. I'm not sure I'm ready for answers about ... anything."

Lucy's hand on her back prodded her gently forward. "It's scary, I know, but you need to understand what's happening to you. Fiona can help."

With a shaky exhale, Shelby nodded. She had never shied away from life's challenges in the past – and there was no reason to start now. Hand trembling only slightly, she knocked on the door's window glass, and in a few moments, Fiona opened it with a serious expression. "Hi there. I'm closed for the day."

"Could we come in for a few minutes?" Lucy asked.

Fiona looked at Shelby, down at the cat, and

back up to Shelby's face. "What's happened?" the woman asked.

Shelby stumbled over her words. "I fell off a ladder today."

Fiona nodded and stepped back so they could come into the warm boutique.

The comforting scents of sandalwood and cinnamon enveloped them. Rune-inscribed candles and stacks of spell books filled one of the shelves. Shelby relaxed slightly, until she noticed Fiona regarding her intently, the woman's keen eyes searching her face.

"You'd better come out back," the woman suggested kindly. With a tilt of her head, she beckoned Shelby and Lucy behind the black velvet curtain separating the store's public and private areas. "Come along, Harper."

For a second, Shelby wondered how Fiona knew the cat's name. She must have told her about the cat one day when she was in the store shopping.

Off the back storeroom, there was a cozy sitting room with a crackling fire and overstuffed armchairs that surprised Shelby. She had pictured bubbling cauldrons, not comfy sofas. Fiona busied herself preparing tea while Lucy prodded Shelby into a cushioned seat.

"Drink this. It will calm you." Fiona pressed a floral teacup into Shelby's tense hands and settled in a chair across from her. The steaming infusion smelled delicate and honey-sweet.

After drinking a fortifying sip and absent-mindedly touching the gem on her necklace, Shelby began haltingly recounting the day's bizarre events – falling off the ladder, the floating book, and being able to hear Harper speaking to her. The words spilled out in a rush, her tone begging Fiona to deliver a reasonable explanation.

The witch listened intently, absently stroking Harper, who had curled up beside her. As Shelby's story wound down, Fiona smiled and nodded.

"What you've experienced is a blessing, not something to fear." At Shelby's doubtful look, she continued, "You've suppressed your gift your whole life, quite subconsciously, but your injury disrupted the walls around your intuition, allowing your abilities to flow freely."

Seeing Shelby about to object, Fiona held up a hand. "I know it's a shock, discovering such power with no warning. The fact is, your sensitivity was always there, an untapped well within. This trauma uncorked the vessel."

Shelby's thoughts whirled as she absorbed this perspective. Could it be true? She had experienced hunches and premonitions since childhood but shrugged them off as coincidence. What if her psychic ability had merely been blocked until now?

"If what you say is true, why did it manifest this way?" Shelby asked slowly. "Why can I suddenly hear my cat and see books floating in the air?"

"You're opening to the energies of this town," Fiona explained. "Hamlet has a rich magical history. The forces at play here amplified your new sensitivity." She leaned forward, her green eyes intent beneath her wavy auburn hair. "You may be able to commune with spirits tied to the land. I suspect one made contact with you at your shop."

Although a shiver danced down Shelby's spine at the memory of invisible hands holding the books, Fiona's words resonated with the truth. Shelby recalled local legends of ghosts lingering to guard buried secrets or rectify old wrongs. What if she could help guide those souls to peace?

Fiona went on, "And as far as being able to hear Harper ... well, the cat is your familiar. Do you know what that is?"

"Not really."

"A familiar is a loyal guardian and a protector. Familiars are psychically connected to witches."

"Witches?" Shelby gasped.

Fiona nodded. "Witch is a word full of different connotations. For now, let's stick to what a familiar is. Familiars are also guides who can help their witches with magic."

"Oh, gosh. I feel like I'm going crazy, but I'm not, right? I'm not losing my mind?" Shelby whispered.

Fiona clasped her hands, smiling. "Not at all. You've been granted a gift - one that might allow you to do great good."

Moved by the witch's compassion and feeling a slight flicker of hope, Shelby managed a shaky smile. She had found not just answers, but acceptance. This gracious woman saw Shelby's ability as something precious, not freakish.

"Your necklace is lovely," Fiona told the young woman. "The stone is rose quartz."

Shelby's hand moved to the gemstone. "My mother gave it to me."

"Did she?" Fiona's head tilted slightly to the side. "Is it a family heirloom?"

"I don't think so."

"Do you know what rose quartz symbolizes?" Fiona asked.

"My grandmother told me it's a healing crystal and a symbol of unconditional love."

Fiona smiled. "She's correct. It also inspires compassion, promotes friendship, love, deep healing, and peace. The stone also deflects negativity and attracts positivity, promotes gentleness and soothing energy, protects, and lowers stress. It is a powerful gemstone."

"I didn't know that." Shelby turned to Lucy, who had intently watched the hour-long exchange between her friend and the psychic while sipping her cooling tea. "Well? What do you think?"

"I think trusting Fiona's guidance is your best move," Lucy said firmly. "You're special. Maybe this town needs someone with your talents."

Gratitude for her wonderful friend washed over Shelby. With Lucy beside her and with Harper's help, she believed she could, with time, learn to accept her new skills, and maybe even use them for something good.

Fiona began collecting the empty mugs, her movements brisk and no-nonsense once again. "You'll need proper training to master your skills. Come see me tomorrow and we'll begin your lessons."

The woman eyed Shelby sympathetically as

uncertainty flickered across the young woman's face. "This is your destiny, child. It will be okay. There's nothing to be afraid of."

Shelby nodded slowly. Her life would never be the same, but change wasn't something to fear. With time and teaching, maybe one day she could wield this power as effortlessly as she ran her bookshop.

Lucy hooked her arm through Shelby's again as they exited the cozy haven of Crow's Crossing back into the bracing night, with Harper following after them. Shelby shivered, burrowing into her coat.

"How are you holding up?" Lucy asked. "Quite a day, huh?"

Shelby huffed a laugh, shaking her head. "That's an understatement. I feel like Alice falling down the rabbit hole into some kind of magical Wonderland, but I think I'm okay." She hesitated. "Mostly okay."

Lucy nodded sympathetically. They walked in silence until Shelby spoke again, her voice barely above a whisper.

"Do you think I could really commune with spirits someday? Even help them find peace?"

The shy hope in her tone made Lucy's heart swell.

"Absolutely. No one knows your capabilities yet -

not even you, but one thing's for certain, I know you'll do wonderful things." Lucy gave her friend a fierce hug.

Shelby clung tightly to Lucy, letting the unconditional support ground her. Familiar buildings and lampposts slid past as they continued up Main Street. The night felt full of possibility now.

When they reached the crossroads, Shelby and Lucy hugged goodnight.

"See you tomorrow." Lucy smiled at her friend.

"Thank you for your help. I don't know what I'd do without you," Shelby told her before parting ways.

Back in Shelby's cozy apartment, Harper leapt lightly onto the young woman's lap, purring loudly. "I need a nap," the cat told her.

Shelby stroked the silky fur, marveling that just hours ago, a talking cat seemed impossible. Now it felt almost natural. Almost.

"We have a lot to learn, you and me," Shelby murmured. The cat blinked up at her with intelligence showing in her eyes.

"The journey is just beginning, but you won't walk it alone," Harper said with sleepy eyes.

Reassured by Harper's comment, Shelby settled

back against the cushions. Her old life was gone, replaced by something rich and strange, frightening and full of potential. She would take it one day at a time.

Glancing around her large, cozy living room, Shelby felt a rush of affection for this place she had called home. Over the years, Hamlet had been transformed too, from a sleepy town steeped in quaint legends to a vibrant town full of artists, musicians, and hints of magic.

She recalled Fiona's words - "This is your destiny" - and shivered. Shelby had never craved power or acclaim, but she did want to help others. If her abilities could provide comfort or closure, then she wouldn't shrink from exploring them.

Tomorrow, her training would begin. Tonight, she would rest and ready her mind. Shelby gave Harper one last lingering scratch under the chin before heading to bed. Curled under the covers, she fell asleep almost instantly with the muffled tolling of the old church bell down the street, chiming like a lullaby.

Her dreams that night were confusing and convoluted ... sensations of falling, finding herself sprawled on the floor, ghosts floating nearby, and being able to chat with Harper.

Morning might bring a few answers and the start of an exciting new chapter, unlike any in the wildest stories Shelby sold at Spellbound Books.

She could hardly wait to turn the page.

4

The next morning, Shelby woke feeling surprisingly rested and calm. Harper lifted her head with sleepy eyes as the young woman got dressed, yawning to reveal a rough pink tongue.

"Ready for an adventure today?" Shelby asked.

The cat blinked, then stretched and hopped gracefully from the bed. "I'm always ready to follow wherever you go."

Harper's words no longer seemed so strange. Shelby smiled as she prepared a quick breakfast for herself and fed her cat. She knew she had a powerful ally in the clever feline.

After eating, Shelby tidied up the apartment and headed downstairs to the bookshop to see if her employee needed anything until she got back.

Assured that the bookstore would be fine for an hour without her, she walked the short distance to Crow's Crossing. Pausing outside the shop, she steadied her nerves before stepping inside.

Fiona looked up from arranging a display of soft knit gloves and beckoned Shelby over. "Welcome, my dear. I'm so pleased you've come back."

She led Shelby and Harper behind the curtain into the cozy sitting room where a fire crackled merrily in the grate. Fiona gestured for Shelby to take a seat while she poured tea.

"How are you feeling this morning?" Fiona asked kindly as she handed Shelby a teacup.

Cradling the warm drink, Shelby considered the question. "Still overwhelmed, but not so afraid anymore. I'm just unsure what to expect."

Fiona nodded. "It's perfectly normal to feel unsettled as your abilities manifest. You'll likely discover more talents in the days, weeks, and months ahead."

Shelby's eyes widened. "More talents? You mean besides hearing cats talk to me and ... and being near ghosts?"

"Oh, yes." Fiona settled into an armchair. "Psychic senses often develop gradually. Yours seem tied to

Hamlet's magical roots. I believe this town enhances your natural gifts."

The psychic smiled at Shelby's thoughtful frown. "Don't worry. I'll teach you to cultivate your skills safely. You're taking the first steps on an incredible journey."

Shelby nodded as she sipped her tea. She felt the tension ease from her shoulders as the liquid's honeyed warmth spread through her. Harper curled up by the hearth, her eyes drifting to half-shut.

"Can you tell me more about familiars?" Shelby asked after a few moments. "Are they spirits themselves, or just animals?"

"A bit of both," Fiona replied. "They're ordinary creatures, but with extraordinary insight. Familiars can see beyond the veil between worlds. They can sometimes share that perception with their human partners through the mental link you now have with Harper."

Shelby considered this, looking down at the drowsing cat's back. "So, she can sense things I can't? She's almost like a spirit guide?"

"Exactly." Fiona smiled. "Your intuition can often speak to you through Harper. Pay close attention to the thoughts and feelings she shares with you."

"I'll keep you informed of any uncanny presences I notice," the cat remarked sleepily, "and warn you of danger when needed."

Shelby nodded, marveling again at their telepathic bond. With Harper's help, she hoped to understand the forces stirring in the town of Hamlet.

Setting her teacup aside, Fiona said, "I think we're ready to start some training exercises. Simple spells today to focus your untapped power."

At Shelby's wide-eyed look, she laughed. "Don't worry, nothing too dramatic. We'll start small."

The woman led the way to a curtained alcove containing a round table draped with purple velvet. Fiona lit a mix of candles in glass jars while Shelby perched uncertainly on one of the chairs.

"Candle magic helps concentrate energy," Fiona explained as she opened a small wooden box and removed several dried lavender sprigs, setting them in a glass dish. "Lavender brings clarity and aids focus."

Shelby watched as Fiona closed her eyes, holding her hands over the flickering candles. The older woman began chanting strange words under her breath that tugged at Shelby's mind. The air felt heavy with power.

After a minute, Fiona opened her eyes and smiled. "Just a simple spell to awaken your inner eye.

We'll build your skills gradually with small rituals like this."

She beckoned for Shelby to place her hands in the air. "Hold your hands over the flames like I did."

Feeling self-conscious, Shelby extended her trembling hands over the dancing candle flames.

"Trust your instincts. Use your breath," Fiona advised. "Let the energy move through you."

Taking a deep breath, Shelby tried to clear her mind. At first she felt awkward trying to remember some of the mystical words Fiona had recited, but as she closed her eyes, she focused on their unfamiliar rhythms and allowed her awareness to drift.

Warmth bloomed in her chest, growing stronger until her whole body hummed with energy. The flames seemed to speak to her - or maybe it was Harper's commentary she heard whispering in her mind. In moments, Shelby felt power swell in her core.

With a long exhale, she opened her eyes slowly. The candles burned a little lower, but the air still shimmered with magic. Shelby turned to Fiona in wonder.

"Did it work?" the young woman asked. "I felt ... something. Like sunbeams moving in my veins."

Fiona nodded. "Excellent. Well done. We'll keep practicing to help you focus that inner light."

They spent the next hour performing various minor spells using candles, stones, and incantations, and bit by bit, Shelby grew a little more confident directing the tingling energy, but she still felt like a complete novice fumbling to understand a new language.

Fiona touched her shoulder reassuringly after one failed attempt. "Don't get discouraged. Skill comes only with time and patience. You have raw talent."

Shelby nodded, trying not to feel disappointed. "This is still so new. I guess I hoped for fast answers."

"And those will come in time." Fiona began tidying up the workspace. "You've made a wonderful start. That's enough for today. It can be very tiring to practice skills."

The woman regarded Shelby with a kind expression. "Go, enjoy the rest of your day. We'll meet again in a few days to continue, but reach out to me if you have a question or concern."

Thanking Fiona, Shelby collected a sleepy Harper into her arms and headed out of the cozy shop. The winter sunlight seemed especially bright after the candlelit dimness indoors. Shelby blinked against the glare, feeling energized despite the mental exertion.

Ambling up Main Street, she turned Fiona's advice over in her mind. Patience and persistence were key. She might want to fully grasp her abilities overnight, but growth would only come gradually.

Glancing down at the cat cradled in her arms, Shelby gave Harper a grateful scratch under the chin. "Well, what do you say we grab a quick lunch at the café before heading back to the bookshop?"

The promise of cream and fish roused Harper from her drowsy state. "Let's hurry before they run out of tuna salad. We can practice more spells later."

Shelby laughed out loud, earning a puzzled look from a passerby. Linking her new secret world with everyday routines would take some getting used to, but with Harper's help, she would figure out how to balance ordinary life with her extraordinary senses.

Each small step brought her closer to understanding the mystical forces stirring in the town she had always called home. Shelby sent up a silent prayer of thanks for her helpers, both human and feline.

Pausing on the sidewalk outside the café, Shelby lifted her face to the winter sunlight, and the warmth of it on her skin seemed to whisper a message.

Don't fear the light within. Let it shine.

"This Christmas ghost tour sounds like fun," Lucy said. "It will get us in the holiday spirit."

Bundled against the cold weather, the two friends set out just after dark to walk the mile to the stately Harris Estate on the outskirts of town. Shelby breathed in the crisp air, enjoying the chance to clear her head after several days spent honing her psychic skills with Fiona's guidance.

Up ahead, the imposing iron gates of the Harris Estate came into view. Evergreen garlands and twinkling lights adorned the entryway, which now bustled with other visitors also eager for some old-fashioned holiday fun.

Shelby gazed at the graceful columns and peaked roofs of the mansion beyond the gates. Even in the gathering darkness, the home's beauty and elegance stood out. It was hard to believe such a refined family once lived with the shadow of witch accusations hanging over them.

"Two tickets for the Candlelight Christmas Ghost

Tour, please," Lucy requested at the ticket booth. After getting their wristbands, she turned to Shelby with bright eyes. "I'm excited to see the holiday decorations inside and hear more about the family ghost."

Shelby smiled, though she felt a prickle of unease thinking about the possibility of encountering the spirit of the long-ago Harris's missing daughter. Shaking off her nerves, Shelby followed Lucy toward the horse-drawn wagon waiting to transport tour groups up to the mansion. She wouldn't let apprehension spoil their evening.

Bundled under blankets, they joined the other eager visitors for the bumpy ride along the wooded lane leading to the sprawling house. Shelby admired the pristine grounds decorated with pine trees and flickering candles along the drive.

There was plenty of time to enjoy the grounds before their tour began so the young women got in line for the Winter Wonderland experience and were soon strolling along the paths with glowing snowmen, a village with small buildings decorated for Christmas and a train winding through them, stands for food and drink, a Santa's Village where elves were making toys, live reindeer at a barn, bonfires, a gift shop, and costumed interpreters walking along wearing 19th-century clothing with capes and singing carols.

"This is beautiful." Shelby's head turned back and forth so she could take in all the decorations and exhibits.

"Want to get a snack?" Lucy suggested as they walked up to a pretty snack shack serving treats.

The friends got hot cider and white-chocolate donuts sprinkled with candy cane pieces. They carried their drinks and donuts to a stage where musicians played holiday tunes.

A few minutes later, two of the young women's friends came by to chat and enjoy the songs.

"This is the best Candlelit Holiday festival they've ever put on," one friend gushed.

"I almost didn't want to come," the other friend told them, "but I'm so glad I didn't miss it."

Realizing the foursome had the same times for the estate tour, they headed over to get in line, and luckily, the line moved fast and they were soon inside the mansion's warmth.

The tour guide - wearing a Victorian-style holiday cape - welcomed everyone and began describing the estate's history. Shelby listened with interest to details about when each wing was constructed and the functions of the formal parlors and libraries. She was impressed by the beautifully decorated interior with wreaths, ribbons, candles, and glittering Christmas trees, making each room festive and inviting.

When their group reached the portrait hall upstairs, Lucy nudged Shelby's arm. "That must be her," she whispered, nodding toward an oil painting of a teenage girl with delicate features and intelligent dark eyes.

Shelby studied the image titled "Prudence" and felt inexplicably sad gazing at the long-ago young woman in her formal gown, standing with a solemn expression. An ornate gold frame highlighted the life she might have known as an adult if she hadn't been accused of witchcraft.

The tour guide cleared his throat, recapturing the group's attention. "And here we have the Harris's only daughter, Prudence. Though not confirmed, many believe her tormented spirit roams these halls looking for her parents."

As the guide continued to describe the supposed supernatural occurrences witnesses had reported over the years, Shelby noticed the candles in the wall sconces sputtering in an odd way.

A faint haze seemed to drift through the hallway,

accompanied by the whisper of something that sounded almost like weeping.

Shelby shivered, her skin prickling.

"Do you feel that, Lucy?" she murmured. "It's so cold in here."

Her friend gave her a puzzled look. "Feel what? It's nice and warm. Maybe you'll warm up soon. We were out in the cold for nearly two hours."

Shelby listened as the guide related a chilling tale of a psychic who had fled the house screaming after making contact with a spirit in the seance room. She frowned, rubbing her hands along the arms of her winter jacket. She realized the inside temperature wasn't actually cold, yet she couldn't shake off the feeling of icy air surrounding her. The sad whispers sounded louder, echoes of grief carried on some otherworldly current only Shelby seemed to sense.

Glancing back at Prudence's portrait, she thought she saw the painted lips move ever so slightly. She blinked hard. *You're imagining things*, she scolded herself. But the heavy atmosphere of sadness still lingered.

The tour guide went on describing the Harris family. After their daughter was accused of witchcraft, she was sent away to Virginia in secret to escape persecution as a witch. The young woman never arrived at her destination and no one knows what happened to her. Penelope and William Harris left Salem and moved to Hamlet, where they settled on this new estate. Originally, the mansion's property consisted of more than twenty acres of land. William opened a merchant store in Hamlet, which was only a mile away from their estate. Penelope and William were bereft when they learned their daughter had never made it to Virginia. They never had more children. Penelope became reclusive and no longer wanted to entertain. Penelope wandered the woods pining for Prudence, wondering if her daughter was dead or alive, and invited psychics to the mansion to try to contact the young woman. Once a joyful man, William lost interest in the things he used to love and became quiet, spending many hours alone in his study."

When their tour moved on, Shelby fell back from the group to walk alone for a few minutes. If some ghostly presence was trying to manifest, she didn't want to distract the other visitors. Shelby kept her gaze fixed straight ahead as more odd noises filtered around her, lights flickered, and a woman's soft cry filled the air. For a second, she smelled the odor of smoke.

Outside once again, she breathed deep gulps of the frosty air, grateful to leave the oppressive sensations in the mansion behind. She paused, debating whether to confide her uneasiness to Lucy or let it go. She was still deciding what to do when her friend turned to her with bright eyes.

"Wasn't that fun?" Lucy bubbled with enthusiasm. "Such amazing holiday decorations, and I almost believe those ghost stories now."

Shelby forced a smile. "Definitely a cool atmosphere," she agreed, not wanting to ruin Lucy's lighthearted mood. "It was fun, but the noises, cries, and flickering lights kind of bothered me."

Lucy looked surprised. "I didn't hear any cries. I didn't notice lights flickering, either."

"I smelled smoke for a few seconds, too."

"Maybe since you hit your head and started developing skills, you're more attuned to sights and sounds," Lucy suggested.

"Could be."

They crunched along the tree-lined lane leading back to the gates, with Lucy happily chattering the whole way. Shelby made occasional responses, but her thoughts preoccupied her. Had the spirit of Prudence Harris been trying to connect with her? And if so, what did she want with her?

Nearing the estate's exit, Shelby hesitated and glanced back. For a fleeting instant, she thought she glimpsed a pale figure framed in an upper window, staring after her. With a shiver, Shelby hurried to catch up to Lucy.

"Everything okay?" Her friend gave her a curious look. "You seem kind of spooked. It was just a fun holiday haunted house tour. I think you're just feeling sensitive after everything that's happened. It's understandable."

"I know, I'm fine." Shelby pushed away the unease still nagging at her. "I just got lost in thought, but you're right. It was really great."

The two friends strolled back into town. Shelby attempted to engage more in Lucy's lively review of every entertaining detail of their evening. By the time they bid each other goodnight, Shelby's mood had lightened.

When she entered her apartment, the cat was sleeping on the sofa. She lifted her head. "Tell me all about it tomorrow. I'm too tired to listen to you now."

Shelby chuckled. "Why do you sleep so much?"

"I'm a cat," Harper reminded her.

Climbing under her covers an hour later, Shelby couldn't stop thinking about all she had sensed at the Harris Estate. Something floated in the air there, something sad, needful, and somehow tied to Hamlet's haunted past. She considered waking Harper to talk things over with her, but she knew the cat wouldn't pay attention in her sleepy state. In a few days, there would be another lesson with Fiona, and Shelby wanted to share her disquieting mansion tour experience with her to see what guidance the wise woman might offer about sensing lost souls.

But that was a mystery for another day. When Shelby clicked off the lamp, the bedroom filled with shadow and Harper snuggled closer. The young woman let the familiar creaks and groans of the old building soothe her as she drifted off to sleep.

5

Shelby woke with a startled gasp and a pounding heart. Flickering images from her dream faded, but a sense of urgency stayed with her. There was something about a fire...

She shook her head, trying to clear the troubling impressions from her mind, but when she met Harper's watchful gaze from the foot of the bed, Shelby hesitated.

"Did you pick up on anything strange during the night?" the young woman asked.

The cat blinked. "It wasn't a dream. A room in the old Harris mansion burned last night," she said.

"What?" Shelby sat bolt upright. "The Harris Estate was on fire? Was it destroyed?"

"No, it wasn't." Harper flicked her tail. "There

was a small blaze in one of the parlors. Luckily, it was spotted and extinguished almost right away, but there was damage to the room."

Shelby sank back against her pillows, stunned. She recalled the acrid, smoky scent in the grand house during last night's holiday tour. When she experienced it, she thought it was her imagination, but now...

"Could I have been sensing the fire before it even started?" she mused aloud. Premonitions were one of the psychic abilities Fiona said might manifest.

Harper looked at Shelby with a steady gaze. "You perceived a tragedy before it occurred. Your powers are continuing to unfold."

Shelby rubbed her forehead. "Was anyone hurt?"

"No one was hurt by the fire. As I said, there was some minor damage to the one room."

With a sigh, Shelby climbed out of bed and headed to the kitchen to make coffee. She had more questions than answers these days. Her deepening connection to Hamlet's supernatural undercurrents felt equal parts frightening and frustrating.

After breakfast, Shelby opened her laptop and soon found a brief article about the fire at the Harris Estate. It had occurred around 11:00 pm just two hours after her and Lucy's evening tour. There were no details about damage or suspected cause, however.

Shelby's forehead crinkled in thought as she got ready to go downstairs to the bookshop. She considered calling Lucy to share her unsettling hunch about the fire but decided against it. Best to keep this new wrinkle to herself for a little while. She'd prefer to talk to Lucy face-to-face.

At Spellbound Books, Shelby busied herself with the usual opening tasks, pushing worries from her mind. When Rachel breezed in later that morning, Shelby welcomed the distraction of hearing about her blossoming romance with the coffee shop cutie.

"Chad is just the sweetest," Rachel gushed as she unpacked a new shipment of young adult novels. "He brought me the most amazing hazelnut latte this morning, and we talked for like an hour."

Shelby smiled, warmed by the dreamy look on Rachel's face. "It's official then. You're totally smitten."

Rachel blushed but looked pleased by her new flame. With Harper napping nearby in a patch of sunlight, the two chatted about books and life while they worked. Shelby felt herself relax, lost in the comforting rhythm of work tasks and laughter with her friend.

Later, while straightening a display shelf, Shelby overheard two women discussing the Harris Estate. She moved closer, straining to catch their conversation.

"What terrible timing, right before their big Christmas season," one woman remarked.

Her companion shook her head. "At least the damage was minor. They don't have to close. They can stay open. I did hear they found remains in the rubble - some poor soul who perished in the fire."

Shelby's breath caught, and she busied herself with arranging the book display again before the women could notice her obvious eavesdropping. So her premonition had signified more than a dangerous blaze. Someone had died in the flames. *But why did Harper tell me the fire didn't hurt anyone?*

The shop's cozy warmth suddenly felt chilling. Shelby rubbed her arms, wishing she had answers about the strange forces that seemed to have plagued the Harris Estate. Were darker presences capitalizing on the tragedy of Prudence Harris? And what did they want from the living? She shook her head and berated herself for letting her thoughts run wild.

The door opened and a tall, good-looking man in a leather jacket stepped inside and glanced around before approaching the counter. "Afternoon. Are you Shelby Price?"

At her wary nod, he pulled a badge from his pocket. "Detective Travis Whitely. I'd like to ask you and a member of your staff a few questions about the Harris Estate fire, if you have a moment."

Shelby stared. Her mouth was as dry as sand. Why did the police want to speak with her about the blaze? Her unease must have shown on her face because the detective hurried to add, "These are just routine inquiries. Several tour groups passed through there yesterday evening. I believe you and your employee Rachel Strand were at the estate last night."

Rachel looked confused but hurried over. "I was there early in the evening with a friend. We took some pictures outside, got a hot chocolate and a pretzel, and then left. We didn't go on the tour."

Shelby took a deep breath and gestured for Detective Whitely to follow her to the employee break room in the back, away from curious customers. She caught Harper's watchful gaze tracking them before the cat leapt down from her perch with ease to trail behind.

Seated at the small table with mugs of coffee, Shelby, feeling tense, waited for the detective to explain his purpose. He flipped open a notebook, his expression serious beneath his tousled dark hair.

"Let's start with your contact information." Once provided, he continued, looking at Shelby. "You went on a holiday tour at the estate last night, correct?"

When Shelby nodded, he asked, "Did you notice anything unusual or out of place during your walk through the mansion?"

Shelby hesitated. Should she mention the frigid pockets of air, echoes of sadness, and the sense of a lurking presence she had attributed to Prudence's ghost? She opted to just shake her head.

Detective Whitely turned his piercing gaze on her. "And nothing struck you as strange or worrisome, Ms. Price?"

Shelby met his eyes for a half-second before dropping her focus to the steaming mug cradled in her hands. "The house has a tragic history. I guess I felt some ... atmosphere in there, but nothing concrete. Just lights flickering and things like that. I'm sure it was part of the tour."

She held her breath as the detective studied her, and after an endless couple of moments, he nodded, and then turned to Rachel.

"Did you notice anything unusual while you walked around the grounds?"

"Nothing. Everything was great," Rachel explained. "People seemed happy."

The detective stood. "I appreciate you taking the time. Here's my contact information if you think of anything that could be relevant."

Shelby walked him to the front door in a daze, head spinning. Why was his focus so intent on her? Could he sense she was holding something back? Thankfully, Rachel had no inkling of Shelby's hidden talents. She just looked a little put out to have her date-gushing interrupted.

"What was that about?" Rachel asked once Detective Whitely had departed. "He didn't really say why he wanted to talk to us."

Shelby shrugged, trying to seem nonchalant. "Routine stuff, I guess. Cops always want to question everyone after an incident. It would be easy to access information about the people who went to the festival at the estate since we had to buy tickets."

Rachel seemed to accept Shelby's explanation, and with a cheerful nod, she returned to unpacking the book shipment. Meanwhile, Shelby spent the rest of the day in a tense fog. Between her psychic hunch before the fire and law enforcement coming to talk to her, she felt certain the fatal fire was about to draw her into something.

At closing time, Shelby said goodnight to Rachel and made her way upstairs, with Harper at her heels. Slumping onto the sofa, she dropped her face in her hands with a groan.

"I don't know what to do, Harper," she confessed. "If my senses can provide clues about threats before they happen, then I feel obligated to act. But how? How could I warn people? They'd think I was a crazy person."

The cat leapt into her lap. "You have a kind heart, but it may be very hard to protect others from darkness. Be patient. Learn about your skills first. Don't push too hard right now."

Shelby sighed, stroking Harper's soft fur. "You're right. Worrying won't help. Maybe Fiona will have some advice for me." She hesitated. "I know Lucy believes in my 'talents,' but should I confide in her about this premonition?" Shelby hated keeping secrets from her oldest friend, but would telling Lucy only make her worry?

"Tell her when you see her in person," Harper advised. "This is a heavy burden made lighter when shared between friends."

Shelby gave a slow nod, seeing the wisdom in Harper's advice. Her friendship with Lucy gave her strength and made her feel calm.

"Why did you tell me no one was hurt in the fire?" she asked the cat.

"Because no one was," Harper told her.

A soft knock at the apartment door made Shelby jump. She wasn't expecting anyone that evening. Peering through the peephole, she was surprised to see Detective Whitely standing on the porch. Shelby stepped back, pulse quickening. What reason could he have for returning?

She took a deep breath and opened the door. "Detective. Did you forget something?" She hoped her voice sounded steady.

His expression seemed almost sheepish. "Sorry to bother you at home, Ms. Price. I just ... had a hunch you might have more to share about the Harris Estate. Intuition, I guess. Can we speak in private?"

Shelby hesitated, then gestured him inside. She watched the detective scan his surroundings before turning his laser-sharp focus on her.

Harper sat grooming herself on the back of the sofa, with a calm and ease that Shelby didn't share.

"Please, have a seat," she offered, and then perched on the edge of the sofa facing him as he settled into an armchair. An odd energy she didn't understand hummed in the air between them.

Detective Whitely seemed to choose his words with care. "Sometimes powerful insights that defy logic come to me during investigations. For example, I can sometimes sense when witnesses omit details on purpose ... details that could prove meaningful." His piercing gaze held Shelby's. "I think you might have additional insights about the fire."

Shelby's mouth went dry. How could this practical detective possibly suspect she had any insight? And yet, his solemn expression held no skepticism.

She glanced helplessly at Harper, who stared at her in response. "Tell him. He is a seeker like yourself."

Swallowing hard and not knowing what the cat meant, Shelby met Detective Whitely's calm gaze. "I believe I ... sensed things at the estate that may be relevant," she began in a halting way. "For a moment, I smelled smoke, but I didn't see any fire at all. My friend and I left before the fire started."

She tensed, expecting disbelief or condemnation for such a silly claim, but the detective simply nodded.

"I wondered if you might have seen or heard something," he said. "It's clear to me that you possess a sensitivity I lack. Please, share anything you noticed during the tour that seemed ... out of the ordinary."

Keeping his eyes on the young woman, he took out a notebook.

Shelby took a steadying breath. At first, she was hesitant, but soon her words spilled out in a rush as she described the cold spots, whispers, flickering lights, and smoke-like mist she had experienced. "It all must have to do with the special effects they use in the mansion. When I smelled smoke, I brushed it off as part of the effects." She paused for a moment. "But maybe it wasn't. Maybe it was ... intuition?"

Detective Whitely was silent for a long moment. "I've learned to trust intangible evidence, however inexplicable." He smiled at Shelby's stunned look. "We all have hidden talents. Yours seem to provide insight beyond facts and figures. Please call me Travis."

"Have the police identified the body that was found in the fire?" Shelby asked.

The detective cleared his throat. "It was a longtime resident of Hamlet. James Peacock, the assistant librarian at the town library."

"Mr. Peacock?" Shelby almost shouted. "Oh no. He was such a nice man. Why would anyone want to kill him?"

The detective gave her a long look. "I didn't say he'd been murdered."

Wringing her hands together and ignoring what the man said, she asked, "Wait. Could it have been an accident? Did Mr. Peacock attend the estate holiday festival that night? Did someone murder him?"

Detective Whitely cocked his head to the side. "It appears Mr. Peacock didn't die in the room where the fire was set. It seems the man was killed somewhere else and brought to the sitting room before the fire started."

"Was the fire set to hide Mr. Peacock's identity?" Shelby questioned.

"The investigation is ongoing. That's all I can say right now." The detective was about to hand Shelby his business card but realized he'd given her one earlier. "Would you mind if I talked to you again?"

Shelby studied him, sensing his sincerity. She managed a little smile.

"I'll help any way I can," she promised.

Detective Whitely grinned and stood to leave. "Thanks for your help," he said. "Sorry to have barged in on you."

After seeing him out, Shelby turned to Harper, her emotions swirling. "He seems kind."

The cat tilted her head. "An interesting man. Perhaps trustworthy. He seems to have a deep intuitive ability, but let's not tell him much about you until we know more about him."

Shelby nodded, considering the note of warning. "Mr. Peacock. Why would anyone want to hurt him? He was always such a pleasant and helpful person. I liked him very much. Maybe it was random?"

"It wasn't random." Harper's tone was firm.

Shelby's eyes narrowed. "Do you know any more about what happened to him?"

"I don't. Not yet."

"What did you mean when you said Detective Whitely is a seeker like me?"

"I sense he has some skills. Maybe it's because he's in touch with his intuition and the world around him ... but maybe it's something more than that. We'll see. Time will tell."

6

Shelby picked at her pasta, too preoccupied to have much of an appetite even though the food was from her favorite Italian place. Across the small table, Lucy watched her with concern.

"You haven't eaten much and you look exhausted. You've got too much going on right now. Maybe paranormal stuff doesn't suit you."

Shelby managed a wan smile at her friend's weak joke. "I know I've been acting weird. I'm sorry. Along with everything else that's happened since I hit my head, I just can't get the fire at the Harris Estate out of my mind." She took a deep breath. "Some strange stuff happened when we were at the holiday festival that night. I think my ... intuition ... was trying to warn me about the danger before it happened."

Lucy's eyes widened, but she leaned forward over the table. "A premonition? Tell me."

With increasing urgency, Shelby described the ominous cold spots, flickering lights, echoes of grief, and the smoke scent that floated around her. "Those things happened hours before the actual fire. I think my senses were picking up clues about the crime before it occurred."

Lucy was silent for a long moment. "If your psychic abilities foreshadowed the fire, that's huge," she told her friend. "Maybe I should hit my head to see if I can develop some powers."

Shelby chuckled.

"Have you told anyone else about this?"

Shelby shook her head. "You're the first. But..." She bit her lip. "Detective Whitely came by the bookshop yesterday to ask me questions. I got the sense he knows I'm holding something back."

"The detective dropped by the inn too," Lucy said with a frown. The young woman worked at a popular Victorian bed and breakfast inn near the center of town. "But he didn't push me for information. He just asked if I noticed anything odd, which I honestly didn't."

Lucy tilted her head. "Travis clearly has you on

his radar, but is that necessarily bad? Maybe having a cop ally would be a good thing."

Shelby considered this as she picked at her cooling pasta. Travis seemed open-minded about her intuition and instincts, and he had come to her for the full story, trusting her to share any impressions she might have had.

But doubt still lingered. Would confiding in law enforcement only make Shelby seem crazy or invite dangerous skepticism? Until she understood more about the forces in play, caution seemed wise.

Lucy's voice broke through her friend's thoughts. "We should go back to the estate. Maybe you could pick up some vibes from the crime scene."

Shelby hesitated, but curiosity won out. She had to know if her senses could unveil clues about the tragedy. "I think it's worth a try," she agreed. "I'll buy us tickets for this weekend's holiday tour."

Saturday evening, the two friends bundled up against the December chill and made the short walk to the Harris Estate. For several minutes, Shelby gazed at the grand home lit up in the darkness. She hoped her psychic radar proved more fine-tuned on this visit. She felt certain there were secrets still hidden in those historic rooms.

People milled about on the sprawling grounds enjoying the festival's rides, music, and food. Shelby wandered around with Lucy letting her intuition guide their steps. She paused when they reached the outdoor skating rink and looked up toward the mansion looming at the top of a small hill.

"That's the wing where the fire broke out, right?" Lucy gestured to an upper-floor window, now dark. Shelby nodded as a chill washed over her that had nothing to do with the cold night air. She sensed they were on the right path.

Nearing the mansion's side entrance, Shelby noticed crime scene tape blocking a service door. With her nerves tingling, she moved closer and noticed soot had blackened the stone around the doorway.

"This must be how the fire fighters accessed the damaged room," she murmured. Glancing around, Shelby pressed her palm to the oak door and felt buffeted by a terrible sense of rage and violence that caused her to sway on her feet.

"Shelby?" Lucy grasped her friend's elbow to steady her. "Are you okay? What happened?"

Shelby took a few deep breaths to clear her head.

"I picked up on some strong emotions. The killer definitely felt overwhelming anger about something. This murder was personal."

Lucy opened her mouth to respond when a tour group approached, and Shelby quickly stepped back from the charred entrance, not wanting to invite questions. She and Lucy blended in with the crowd filing into the mansion's main hall to start the guided walkthrough.

Shelby tried to keep her psychic channels shut off as they proceeded through the festively decorated rooms, not wanting to risk another overwhelming flood of sensations, but she scrutinized every inch of the hall, hoping for clues that might have eluded investigators.

Their group paused in a portrait gallery and Shelby's attention was drawn toward a landscape painting. It showed a moonlit grove of pine trees almost like something from a fairytale. She stepped closer, struck by a nagging familiarity.

"What is it?" Lucy whispered. "Do you feel something about that painting?"

Although Shelby shook her head, she couldn't tear her gaze away from the tranquil scene. Some vital clue seemed to lurk there just beyond her grasp. Before she could figure it out, their guide herded the group forward again. Shelby cast a last frustrated glance back at the puzzling artwork.

At last, they reached the area near the grand upper parlor that had sustained fire damage. Peeking through a crack in the door into the sitting room, Shelby's breath caught at seeing the elegant room's scorched walls and boarded-up windows. Caution tape formed a barrier across the arched entry.

As the guide began describing the tragic discovery of the victim's body, Lucy whispered to Shelby, "Let's slip away. We need to investigate the room alone. I bet we can get in with no one seeing us if we access it through that service door we saw outside."

Shelby's eyes widened, but Lucy was already breaking away from the group. With a last nervous scan to ensure they weren't being observed, Shelby followed her friend out to the hallway. Neither spoke as they hurried down the huge main staircase and slipped out a side door.

The cold night air was a shock after being in the stuffy mansion. Lucy waved Shelby over to a shadowy alcove by the blocked-off doorway they had found earlier.

Shelby perceived the angry male energy again

and she fought to push past the rage to focus on specifics. Had jealousy fueled the brutal act? Vengeance? A love triangle?

She glanced at the door and swallowed hard. The killer must have accessed the upstairs room through this side entrance. Shelby hesitated, afraid to enter the mansion through the side door. *What if someone sees us and we get into trouble? What if the awful sensations I feel get worse? What if...?*

Before she could decide what to do, the heavy door abruptly swung outward. Shelby leapt back with a startled yelp as she saw Detective Whitely's tall silhouette filling the doorway, his flashlight blinding them in the darkness.

"This area is restricted," he said sharply. Then recognition dawned. "Ms. Price?"

Shelby froze like a deer in the headlights under the flashlight's glare. She opened and closed her mouth, unable to form any excuse for being near an active investigation scene.

Travis surveyed them both with raised eyebrows. "What's going on? Why are you here?"

The two friends exchanged looks. Busted.

Shelby's cheeks burned in the darkness. She felt like a foolish child caught sneaking forbidden candy before dinner.

What had possessed her to think she could get away with psychic sleuthing right under the noses of law enforcement? She must have hit her head harder than she realized if she imagined Travis would be anything but angered by her interference.

Lucy tried to come up with a plausible excuse. "Since we had such a good time here the other night, we decided to come back to the festival."

The detective raised an eyebrow. "I don't believe this side of the mansion is on the tour."

"We were snooping around," Shelby admitted. "We liked Mr. Peacock. He was a nice man. It's hard to believe someone would kill him. We're trying to make sense of his murder."

After several seconds, Travis nodded. "Follow me." He opened the door and walked through a dark hallway to a steep staircase. At the top of the stairs, they entered the main part of the mansion. He opened a door and before they walked inside, he warned, "Don't touch anything."

In the fire-ravaged parlor, Shelby winced at the damage. Splotches of soot scarred the once elegant wallpaper, molten globs of wax from candles dotted the charred hardwood floor, and the richly embroidered chairs and curtains had suffered significant damage.

Detective Whitely faced the young women. "How well did you know Mr. Peacock?"

His stern tone alarmed Shelby, but looking closer, she realized he seemed more curious than angry. She drew a shaky breath.

"I grew up in Hamlet. Mr. Peacock knew a lot about the town. I met with him several times to learn more about the history," she admitted. "We're not trying to interfere with the investigation or get in your way. We just wondered if there was some way we could help."

The detective studied her before flicking his gaze to Lucy who nodded in agreement.

"Shelby is very intuitive. She has good reasoning skills. She often sees things that others overlook," her loyal friend explained. Lucy lifted her chin as if daring Travis to contradict her.

The man nodded, and a long moment passed before he spoke.

"I try to stay open to all paths that could lead to information, even unorthodox ones." His tone turned wry. "Clearly, you two plan to insert yourselves into the investigation. Here are a few ground rules you have to follow or you might end up getting arrested for hindering an ongoing investigation: don't get in law enforcement's way, don't put yourselves in danger, and if you discover anything that seems important, then you need to tell me right away."

Shelby flushed, but his expression held no anger.

"Look around the room," he requested. "Do you see anything of interest?"

Shelby took a deep breath to calm her nerves. The room was heavy with negative emotions. "There was a lot of rage in this room." Something picked at her. Something was off, but she didn't know what it was.

Detective Whitely listened, his gaze never leaving her face. "A revenge attack? That might fit with Mr. Peacock's background. He put away some dangerous criminals as a prosecutor before retiring. What makes you think there was a lot of rage in here?"

Shelby couldn't admit to feeling the emotions still floating on the air. "Well, you told me Mr. Peacock was killed elsewhere and brought here to this room. Despite setting the body on fire, there are chairs overturned and the drapes over there look like they were pulled down from the rods. Fire wouldn't do those things so if the man was dead before he was placed here, there couldn't have been a fight between the victim and the killer that would result in chairs tipping over and drapes being pulled down. The killer must have had a fit in here before he set the body on fire."

Detective Whitely looked surprised by Shelby's assessment. "That makes a lot of sense. You have strong powers of observation. That said, I want to give you some advice. You both need to stop pursuing this on your own. Leave it to law enforcement. No more amateur sleuthing - it's too risky."

Seeing Shelby about to object, he held up a hand. "However, I might be able to use your help. You seem to have some unique insight that could be useful to the investigation. If I have something for you to look at, I'll get in touch. For now, please enjoy the rest of your night." He smiled slightly. "And stay out of blocked-off rooms."

Shelby returned his smile, still somewhat dazed by this turn of events. "We will, and thank you, Detective."

"That hallway will return you to the public part of the mansion." The detective shut and locked the parlor, then nodding at both of them, Travis turned briskly and strode away.

Lucy turned an awestruck look on Shelby.

"He totally thinks you can help." She hugged her

friend. "You're gonna help crack a real-life murder case with your super-senses."

Shelby laughed as relief bubbled up to displace her anxiety. "He probably said that stuff to placate us ... make us feel like we can help him so that we stop looking into things on our own. But if he is serious, let's just hope I can control these powers enough to contribute something useful."

Shelby looked back at the closed parlor door. "Something feels off, but I don't know what it is."

Lucy linked arms with her friend. "You'll figure it out. Just trust those psychic skills of yours."

Shelby smiled at her friend's confidence in her. For now, a possible alliance with Detective Whitely was more than she could have hoped for.

Stepping out into the starry night, Shelby tipped her face up to the sky. The full moon seemed to wink down at her, giving her a celestial seal of approval. Feeling lighter than she had in days, Shelby fell into step beside her best friend and partner-in-investigation.

7

The vision came to Shelby in fragments - a flash of a winter jacket, wisps of white hair, the scent of old books and newsprint, a light on in a home office.

She tossed restlessly unable to grasp the meaning behind the disjointed impressions as she hovered between sleep and waking. With a gasp, her eyes flew open and she bolted upright in bed. As the early morning light filtered around the edges of the window blinds, Shelby pressed a hand to her racing heart, her skin feeling cold and clammy.

"It was just a dream," she muttered to herself, but an ominous feeling that something wasn't right still gripped her. Glancing down, she met Harper's green-eyed gaze.

"Did you pick up on anything while I slept?"

Shelby asked. "I had an unsettling dream about Mr. Peacock."

The cat said, "Your unease is warranted. The waters are still murky regarding that poor gentleman's fate."

Shelby sighed. When she'd heard Mr. Peacock had perished in the Harris Estate fire, she'd experienced profound regret that her psychic senses hadn't allowed her to prevent the tragedy. She'd smelled smoke at the mansion and hadn't reported it. Maybe remnants of that guilt had seeped into her subconscious.

But she couldn't ignore the persistent dread swirling in the pit of her stomach. Her intuition was sending muddled but urgent warnings. Something wasn't what it seemed.

She threw back the covers. "I need to clear my head. Let's go for a walk."

Harper rose and, leaning on her front legs, the cat stretched her back before following the young woman out the door.

Bundled against the frosty morning air, Shelby headed toward the picturesque lane of Victorian cottages on the edge of town. She knew the charming light blue house halfway down the block belonged to - *had* belonged to - the late Mr. Peacock.

Shelby slowed as the lovely home came into view. Yellow tape sealed the front door. She felt a pang of grief welling in her heart at the loss of the kind gentleman who had delighted in sharing his knowledge of local history with her.

Harper looked up at her owner. "The dwelling holds information. We should investigate further."

Spurred by Harper's prompt and her own feeling of unease, Shelby nodded. She didn't think anyone would mind if she just took a quick peek around the premises.

Moving up the walkway, Shelby edged along the side of the home cupping her hands against the windows to peer inside. The cozy interior looked tidy and well- furnished. She saw no signs of a disturbance or struggle.

Rounding the far corner, Shelby pulled up short at the sight of a man bent to examine some trampled shrubbery along the side fence. Heart leaping into her throat, she stumbled backwards and collided with a trash can, sending it crashing over.

The figure spun, eyes widening. "Oh! Shelby. Are you all right? You gave me quite a fright."

Shelby stared, certain she was still dreaming because she was seeing the impossible. Mr. James Peacock stood before her in his winter jacket and gloves, very much alive. A small suitcase stood on the walkway nearby.

"Mr. Peacock?" she choked out. "You're ... not dead?"

He blinked at her, bewildered. "Not last I checked, though I had a bit of a cough a day ago."

Shelby's thoughts reeled. How could this be? The body found at the estate ... the murder ... none of it made sense now.

She was vaguely aware of Harper rubbing at her ankles. Drawing a shaky breath, Shelby forced her whirling mind to focus.

Harper said, "Tell him before he thinks you're nuts."

"Mr. Peacock, I'm so glad you're all right. I'm just ... shocked." Shelby scrambled to her feet and her words spilled out as she explained there had been a murder in town and that the police thought he had been the victim. "The police found your wallet on the deceased."

"My gosh," Mr. Peacock said. "I had no idea. I was so busy, I hadn't been paying attention to the news." He gestured to the shrubbery. "I just got home. I took a ride share from the train station. I noticed the shrubbery had been trampled. See there?"

"The intruder may have done that," Shelby suggested.

"Oh, I see. Maybe we should go inside? I should call the police."

"That's a good idea."

Mr. Peacock bustled Shelby and the cat indoors while politely ignoring the young woman's stumbling steps and astonished stares. He put on a kettle for tea before settling across from her at the kitchen table.

"Forgive the mess," he said. "I've been away at a writer's conference. The trip was rather last-minute, so I'm afraid I left the house in disarray."

Shelby leaned forward, listening in disbelief as Mr. Peacock described being invited to present at a conference in New York City. In his excitement over the unexpected opportunity, he had raced off without telling anyone where he was going, forgetting his wallet and cell phone on the kitchen counter.

"I did have my passport with me and an extra credit card. It was a very interesting conference," he admitted. "I enjoyed presenting my article on writing fiction after a career penning many non-fiction legal pieces. The event only lasted four days, and when it was over, I took the first train back."

He opened a biscuit tin and offered a butter cookie to Shelby. "With no phone, I didn't get any messages about my supposed demise. What an unbelievable misunderstanding. I assumed I'd return to a stack of mail on my doorstep, not police tape."

Shelby shook her head, still struggling to reconcile the improbable situation with the murder investigation she had been so involved in the past few days.

"The police found a body in a fire at the Harris Estate," she explained. "They identified him as you because your wallet was on the body. I guess the dental records and DNA testing hadn't come back yet. I just can't believe the mistake."

Mr. Peacock nodded in understanding. "A terrible tragedy regardless of the victim's identity, but I, however, remain hale and hardy." He chuckled then, eyes twinkling behind his spectacles. "Rather amusing to be present for one's own eulogies." His expression turned serious. "Who was the poor man who was killed? He was in my house? The man must have stolen my wallet. Why were the victim and the killer in my house?"

Shelby shook her head. "I have no idea." Mistaken identity or not, a brutal crime had still occurred and the killer likely believed his vendetta had been accomplished, unaware his true target was still alive. She shuddered at the unsettling thought knowing the killer would probably try again.

Abruptly, the front door rattled as someone knocked on it.

When Shelby jumped, Mr. Peacock pushed to his feet. "Well, I'd better see who's on my porch then."

Before Shelby could object, the man hurried to the front hall and opened the door partway, peering out to the porch. She held her breath, her ears straining to hear who it was. Had the murderer returned? She stood and waited.

But the only sound was a jovial voice exclaiming, "Jim, you old goat! The whole town heard you'd passed. I was walking past the house and saw you in the window."

"It was a mistake." Mr. Peacock laughed aloud. "I'm still kicking, though doctors say I ought to lay off the brandy." He swung the door wide to admit a portly, bearded gentleman Shelby vaguely recognized from around town.

"Allow me to introduce my friend, Professor Jeffrey Rundle," Mr. Peacock announced. "An expert on medieval religious texts, though his true passion is the golf course, I daresay."

Professor Rundle pumped Mr. Peacock's hand enthusiastically. "You can't imagine the stir your supposed demise caused, but it's wonderful to see it's been grossly exaggerated."

He turned a genial smile on Shelby. "And who might you be, my dear?"

"I'm Shelby Price. I run the bookshop on Main Street." She stood there awkwardly shifting from foot to foot. "I stopped by to check on Mr. Peacock's, um, house."

"Of course, of course. Terrible confusion all around," Professor Rundle declared. "But Jim seems no worse for wear. I'd best let you recover from all the chaos. Do call if you need anything."

With more lively hand shaking and back-slapping, the professor left the house. Mr. Peacock waved before closing the door and turning to Shelby.

"Jeffrey can be a pompous windbag, but he's harmless. Well, my goodness, what a morning."

Shelby managed a weak smile, trying to hide the fact that her equilibrium was still tilting. She had gone from believing Mr. Peacock murdered to finding him outside his cozy home inspecting the shrubbery. She felt like she could use a huge mug of coffee after all of the shocks.

"I should let Detective Whitely know you're alive

and well," she ventured. "He'll need to ... reassess some things." *Like an entire homicide investigation*, she thought to herself.

"Splendid idea." Mr. Peacock bustled about the kitchen. "Please convey my sincere apologies for the confusion. I look forward to providing any help in unraveling this mess."

Still dazed, Shelby looked down at her cat, and Harper brushed against her leg, gazing up with a look of sympathy.

"Quite the unexpected twist," the cat remarked, "but very fortunate that no actual harm came to this gentleman."

"Right..." Shelby murmured. She pulled out her phone with hands still faintly trembling. Best to update the detective on the shocking new development right away.

The detective arrived in under fifteen minutes, looking sharp and professional in his dark overcoat. Travis was unable to hide his astonishment when Mr. Peacock greeted him at the door. Soon the three of them were sitting around the kitchen table as Mr. Peacock related his tale.

"A case of mistaken identity then," Travis mused, shaking his head in wonder and turning to look at Shelby for a moment. "An innocent man died. It just wasn't you, sir." He regarded Mr. Peacock as he spoke in a somber tone, "You're very fortunate. Your reputation as a prosecutor made you an obvious target for anyone harboring a grudge."

Mr. Peacock removed his spectacles and polished them as he thought about what the detective said. "I did put away some dangerous characters during my career, but I can't fathom who would go to such lengths now, after I've been retired for a few years."

"We'll need you to review a list of former inmates and clients," Travis said. "See if any names jump out."

"I'd be glad to."

"Someone must have broken into your house while you were away. The intruder must have pocketed your wallet and phone," the detective mused. "The killer probably came in while the intruder was still here. Thinking it was you, he murdered the man."

"How unbelievably terrible." With sad eyes, Mr. Peacock shook his head. "But the question remains … why is someone after me?"

"Is there someone you could stay with for a while?" the detective asked. "It might be better not to be alone."

Mr. Peacock considered the suggestion. "I would prefer to stay in my home. I'll think about it."

"Let me know what you decide to do." The detective stood and offered his hand. "For now, stay alert. Whoever killed that man likely thinks his mission has been accomplished, but when he hears the news that you're still alive, he might return. Be aware of your surroundings. Call the police emergency line if anything seems off."

After a nod at Shelby and a final bemused shake of his head, the detective left the house. Shelby lingered for a moment, feeling a sense of profound relief. She hadn't been able to prevent the senseless death, but at least Mr. Peacock was still alive and grateful for missing a brush with a mortal attack. Vowing to herself that when her intuition screamed a warning, she would find a way to intervene before the darkness claimed a victim.

After she bid Mr. Peacock a fond farewell, the man bustled off to brew a fresh pot of tea. Back outside in the brisk air, Shelby turned a thoughtful gaze up to the clear blue sky.

"Why do I feel like we just stepped through the looking glass?" she wondered aloud as her boots crunched over the light covering of snow on the sidewalk.

"Because we just did." Harper peered up at her.

"Your dream and senses led the way past the smoke and mirrors of mistaken identity."

The corners of Shelby's mouth turned up. "So, you're saying I should trust my instincts, even when the facts seem against them."

The cat blinked her approval. "You should. Your heart holds wisdom, if you're ready to listen to it."

With a nod, Shelby turned her steps toward home and the cozy bookshop waiting for her. The world felt like it was aligning into focus again after several days of distortion.

But dangerous illusions still waited in the shadows. The peace of Mr. Peacock's reprieve was only temporary if the killer remained undiscovered. Sobered by the thought, Shelby quickened her pace.

She had work to do.

8

The cozy bookshop windows glowed invitingly against the frosty night outside. Shelby hummed softly to herself as she worked, appreciating the peace and quiet after the shock of recent events. The warmth from the crackling fireplace warmed her and made the space cozy and inviting.

Glancing at the clock, she saw it was almost 8pm. Shelby had decided to keep the shop open longer in hopes of catching some late-evening holiday shoppers.

Soon she was lost in the soothing rhythm of her tasks - straightening book piles, dusting shelves, wiping smudges from the front window. Her mundane chores never felt like drudgery. She loved her bookshop, a place filled with stories that sparked the imagination. She added some books to the circular table by the door where the staff recommendations were displayed. Shelby's suggestion was *To Kill A Mockingbird* by Harper Lee, whom Harper the cat was named after.

The cheerful jangle of the bell over the door announced a new arrival, interrupting Shelby's thoughts. She turned with a welcoming smile that widened when she saw her visitor.

"Lucy! I'm so glad you came by."

Shelby's closest friend unwound a vibrant red scarf from her throat as she hurried over, cheeks flushed from the cold. "I was hoping you'd still be open. I worked late at the B and B so I thought I'd stop in and see how you're holding up after, well, everything."

Since calling Lucy that morning with the shocking news that Mr. Peacock was alive, Shelby's world had tilted back into some semblance of normalcy, but she welcomed Lucy's company after the upheaval of the recent days.

"I'm doing okay. I still feel a bit unsettled, but I'm so relieved that Mr. Peacock is alive," Shelby admitted as she prepared steaming mugs of cinnamon tea while Lucy made herself at home in one of the plush armchairs near the fireplace.

Soon the two friends were deep in discussion about the latest improbable twist. Harper leapt gracefully onto Shelby's lap and settled there. Gazing into the dancing flames, Shelby absently stroked the cat's sleek fur as she turned things over in her mind.

"Mr. Peacock is still in danger," she said slowly to her friend. "The real killer is still out there, thinking his vendetta is complete. The news about the case of mistaken identity and that Mr. Peacock is alive is all over the media outlets. It won't be long before the killer finds out and comes back to attack Mr. Peacock." Despite the fire's warmth, an icy chill swept through Shelby's body at the thought that Mr. Peacock was in danger.

Lucy nodded, looking troubled. "You're right, the good news is only temporary. Any idea why someone would want to target the man? Maybe old grudges from his lawyer days?"

Shelby rubbed the back of her neck thoughtfully. "I think we should do some digging into his background. Maybe we can identify someone from the past who might have cause to wish him harm."

"Detective Travis told us not to go sleuthing on our own anymore," Lucy pointed out wryly.

Shelby waved a dismissive hand. "Research isn't

sleuthing. We're just ... concerned citizens trying to assist law enforcement." Her eyes held a determined glint.

"Okay, where do we start this research?" Lucy asked, matching Shelby's resolute tone. "We can access newspaper archives through the town's library database."

Shelby nodded approvingly. "Old articles about Mr. Peacock should give us some background. Maybe a former client with a grudge will jump out at us." Her eyes widened. "I didn't mean that literally."

"I know." Lucy laughed.

They moved to the sofa and huddled around Shelby's laptop while the young woman tapped at the keys. Pages of information about James Peacock came up; and many of the articles mentioned what a hardworking and dedicated lawyer he'd been in his pursuit of justice as a prosecutor.

"There are plenty of cases of his with defendants who would be enraged by the outcome of the trials. It's like looking for a needle in a haystack." Shelby stifled a yawn, the long day catching up with her.

Lucy yawned too, then stood and stretched, glancing at her watch. "I should get home. I have an early morning tomorrow." She hugged Shelby tightly. "Call me if anything else weird happens, okay?"

"Don't worry, you'll be the first to know." Shelby smiled.

After walking her friend to the door and turning the rectangular card to "Closed," Shelby returned to the comfort of the armchair, gazing pensively into the dying fire. She ought to close up for the night, but her racing thoughts kept her anchored near the hearth, turning over angles and suspicions about the tragic events plaguing her little town.

A faint draft raised the fine hairs on Shelby's arms, even though the fire still radiated warmth. She glanced up with a frown, sensing a change in the atmosphere. An unnatural coolness permeated the cozy space. Shelby shivered, goosebumps prickling her skin as she looked around for the source of the temperature shift.

Don't tell me the furnace went out, she thought to herself.

Before she could walk over to check the thermostat, a shimmer in the air beside the front counter caught Shelby's eye. She watched, transfixed, as faint sparkles began swirling faster and faster suddenly congealing into a see-through form. The apparition of a woman took shape, and she was staring right at Shelby.

With a gasp, Shelby stumbled backward. The ghost flickered but held her insubstantial shape. She wore a vintage light blue dress and her pale blonde hair was styled in rolls, a fashion from decades past. The spirit drifted a little closer.

With her heart pounding, Shelby forced herself to stand her ground, but no malice emanated from the ghost hovering before her; only peace, patience, and an aura of melancholy.

Slowing her breathing, Shelby tried to use her new psychic powers to probe the ghost's energy, but her thoughts were so jumbled she couldn't concentrate.

"What is that?" she whispered to the cat.

"You know what it is. It's a ghost," Harper replied.

"What is she doing here?"

"She lives here in the bookshop," the cat explained.

Shelby's eyes widened. "Since when?"

"Since she died."

"Why?"

"She used to own this building."

"Will she talk to me?"

"Probably not. She only talks to me."

"What's her name?" Shelby asked.

"Emily. Emily Harris."

Shelby took a quick look at the cat. "Is she related to the Harris family who used to own the estate?"

"She is a very distant relative of theirs from George Harris' brother's side."

"Why does she stay here? Isn't she lonely?"

"It's complicated," the cat informed her.

The apparition gave Shelby an almost sad smile, and then the diaphanous form began dissolving with her sparkling atoms scattering into the shadows.

"Wait - don't go!" Shelby cried; her hand outstretched as if she could restrain the specter by using her will, but the ghost vanished as soundlessly as she had appeared.

The shop's temperature abruptly returned to normal again with the spirit's departure. Shelby realized Harper was pressing against her leg and she reached down to stroke the cat's back.

"It's all right. I'm fine," she murmured.

Harper gazed up at her solemnly. "The spirit means you no harm. She's tied to this place."

"For how long?" Shelby asked.

Harper headed for the hearth. "Until she decides she isn't."

Shelby sank slowly back into the armchair, leaning her head against the cushioned seatback. "How has this become my life? Talking cats, a man who isn't dead after all, premonitions and psychic thoughts, and now a ghost." She looked at Harper. "Why reveal herself to me now?"

"Because you can see her now." Harper settled on the hearth, wrapping her plumed tail neatly around her paws. "She's the shop's founder," the cat explained. "Her spirit never strayed far, watching over the store she built and all those who have come in here. She waits to be remembered."

"Remembered? What does that mean?" Shelby repeated in wonder.

"Only she knows why she lingers."

Shelby knew the bookshop had changed hands many times before she took ownership, but she never thought to investigate who originally established the shop almost a hundred years ago.

Shelby closed her eyes, picturing the quiet, lovely ghost. In life, she must have tended this place and its patrons with care. She and Emily were like kindred souls tied together across the many years that separated them by their dreams of owning a shop.

When she opened her eyes, Shelby recalled something. She stood and crossed briskly to the back shelves of the storeroom that held boxes of things from the shop's past. Rifling through the memorabilia, she soon found what she remembered seeing when she first bought the place - a black and white photograph of the front interior from decades ago.

A pretty young woman stood behind the checkout counter, her smile bright and engaging. The woman had the same delicate features and wavy blonde hair as the ghost.

Shelby gently set the photo on the mantel. "You're home, Emily," she whispered. "We'll remember you."

She lingered before the image of the past - Emily immortalized in her prime, in her lovely shop.

With a smile, Shelby moved slowly about the shop turning off the lights and the lamps, and then went to check that she'd locked the front door where she paused to press her palm against its sturdy wood. So many hands had touched that wood. So many people had spent time in the shop. She could almost feel the steady rhythm binding the past and the present.

Beside her, the cat asked, "Ready to head upstairs?"

Shelby smiled down at her faithful companion. "Let's get some rest. We have lots to do tomorrow."

Harper purred and looked up at Shelby with what almost looked like a smile.

9

Shelby hummed along to the holiday music playing softly in the background as she inventoried the new shipment of books. The cozy bookshop was still and peaceful this early on a wintry morning. Harper dozed in a patch of sunlight near the front window, guarding the entrance against intruders.

The cheerful jangling of bells announced the arrival of Patrice Nelson, another member of the shop's staff. Shelby smiled warmly at the petite older woman who removed her winter coat and gloves.

"Welcome back, Patrice. We missed you. How was your visit to Tucson to see your son and your grandkids?"

"It was absolutely wonderful. The weather was beautiful. My son and daughter-in-law took me to a few museums, we went hiking, and had some delicious meals." Patrice leaned over to give Shelby an affectionate hug. "The little ones have grown so much. We were so happy to spend time with them, but it's always nice to be back home."

Shelby nodded understandingly. Except for her college years, she had never lived anywhere but Hamlet, surrounded by history and family. The charming town was in her blood.

While Patrice bustled behind the front counter, stowing away her coat and purse, Harper jumped up on the counter to greet the woman. "And how is this beautiful cat? I missed seeing you." She patted Harper's luxurious fur. "Anything exciting happen while I was away?" The woman paused and looked at Shelby. "You know, we saw two police cars at James Peacock's house last night when we drove into the neighborhood after landing in Boston."

Shelby quickly filled in her co-worker on the shocking mistaken identity surrounding Mr. Peacock and the tragic fire victim found at the Harris Estate. Patrice's blue eyes widened behind her stylish glasses.

"Good heavens. What a dreadful mix-up. I'm so relieved James is all right, but that poor man who was killed." She shook her head sorrowfully. "Did they determine who the victim was?"

"Not yet." Shelby kept her voice low, conscious of early customers browsing the shelves. "I bet the police were just doing routine follow-ups when they visited Mr. Peacock again last night. I bet that's all it was." Despite her reassuring words, she felt a chill of worry slip over her skin. She was concerned that investigators had discovered a new threat, but she didn't want to alarm Patrice. She needed to know more and there was no point in speculating.

Patrice clucked sympathetically as she straightened a display of holiday-themed fiction books. "It's no wonder Jim might attract danger, considering his career. So many criminals saw him as the enemy."

Shelby perked up. Because Patrice and her husband Ron were long-time friends of Mr. Peacock's, the woman might have insights into his legal career and any enemies he might have acquired over the years.

Casually resuming her task of unpacking books, Shelby asked, "Did Mr. Peacock ever mention anyone in particular who held a grudge against him? Maybe a former defendant out for revenge?"

Patrice looked thoughtful as she efficiently processed new inventory into the computer system.

"You know, there were a few defendants whose behavior seemed dangerously unhinged at trial. One man screamed threats at Jim in the courtroom after being sentenced." She shook her head. "But that was years ago, and I'm nearly certain that awful man is still behind bars. Jim would remember better than I do who might wish him harm."

Shelby nodded, disappointed not to gain any solid leads but glad Mr. Peacock hadn't shared concerns about being targeted over old professional grudges. Maybe the danger came from a more recent source.

The conversation was put on hold as Patrice helped a customer find the books on their wish list and Shelby returned to cataloging inventory. Watching the woman greet patrons with warm familiarity, Shelby felt a rush of affection for her little shop's tight-knit community. As she worked, her thoughts circled back to worries over Mr. Peacock's safety. Shelby couldn't suppress the creeping unease that the killer would return. She hoped Detective Whitely would update her on the reason the police made another visit to the man's home last night.

Near noon, Shelby was restocking cookbooks when the front door burst open, the bell overhead rattling. Detective Whitely strode in looking grim, and his gaze landed on Shelby.

"I need to speak with you about James Peacock. There was an incident at his home last night."

Shelby paled. "Is he all right?"

Travis hesitated for a second before replying quietly, "He's fine. Some unusual activity was reported in his backyard late last night. He thought he saw someone walking back there. He called the police to report it, and the officers found footprints in the fresh snow near his porch. We're concerned that the killer learned Mr. Peacock was alive and may have returned to the house last night."

Shelby's breath caught. She shared a tense look with Travis. It seemed the killer hadn't given up on his quest.

"We kept a police car outside the house for the rest of the night," the detective told her, "but we don't have the resources to do that every night."

Patrice heard what the detective had said and gripped the checkout counter tightly. "How awful. That poor man, having to live in fear." She turned to the detective with worried eyes. "What can be done to keep Jim safe?"

"We've increased patrols in his neighborhood. I know you and your husband are some of his closest friends, so please call me if you notice anything suspicious that could be relevant."

Patrice nodded and went to get her phone. "I'm going to call my husband to tell him what's going on."

"Has the dead man been identified yet?" Shelby asked the detective.

"Not yet, but I'm expecting the information to come in sometime today. Knowing who the victim is might help us to identify some suspects."

"Why would the killer take the body to the Harris estate?" Shelby asked. "Why didn't he just set Mr. Peacock's house on fire with the body in it? Why take the risk of moving the body to the estate especially with the winter holiday festival going on?"

The detective let out a long sigh. "That's what I've been trying to figure out."

With butterflies swirling in her stomach, Shelby stepped out of the bookshop into the frosty late afternoon air, leaving the shop in Patrice's capable hands. After the unsettling visit from Detective Whitely, she felt she needed to seek guidance from the one person who would understand her concerns – Fiona, the psychic.

With Harper trotting loyally beside her, Shelby hurried down the slushy sidewalks along the cobblestone main street to the witch's popular boutique. Shelby peered into the windows as she approached, reassured to see the lights on.

The door's bells tinkled as Shelby entered the pretty store. As always, the cozy space soothed her worries with its soft music, colorful artwork, and beautiful clothes and jewelry.

Fiona came out from behind the curtained doorway, looking every bit the mystic in flowing layers of purple and silver, and her auburn hair tumbling wildly about her shoulders. Her wise eyes were warm and welcoming.

"Shelby, my friend. This is a pleasant surprise." Fiona studied the young woman closely. "I sense heavy thoughts are weighing on you. Please, come to my office and sit by the fire."

In a few minutes, Shelby settled in a soft velvet armchair, clutching a delicate teacup as she gathered her swirling thoughts. Harper nestled comfortably on Fiona's lap, eyes drifting contentedly half-shut under the witch's gentle strokes.

As Shelby spoke, her words were hesitant.

"When I first came to see you, you said my abilities might one day help guide lost souls and protect the innocent." She raised her eyes to the woman. "Someone is in danger, and I feel powerless to help."

Fiona regarded the young woman solemnly, waiting for Shelby to continue.

Taking a fortifying sip of the fragrant tea, Shelby described the latest developments - the stalker at Mr. Peacock's home and the murderer still on the loose.

"I want to keep people safe, but I don't know how to use these skills for more than vague premonitions," Shelby concluded helplessly. She shook her head, frustration welling. "You help me understand my gifts. How can I master them enough to do some real good? How do I protect Mr. Peacock and help find the killer?"

Fiona considered her words before responding. "Your desire to protect is admirable, but don't let urgency make you act rashly." She held Shelby's gaze intently. "Developing your talents requires time, patience, and care. The path ahead remains clouded - you must let it unfold in its own time. You can't push skill development. Every skill takes time and experience to improve."

Shelby bit her lip, tamping down the desperation

swelling in her chest. As much as she wanted concrete answers, she respected the witch's wisdom.

Fiona continued gently, "I know you seek to understand your purpose, but the way is seldom clear at first. Nurture the seeds of skill I helped you plant. Growth emerges slowly but surely when the conditions are right."

Closing her eyes, Shelby ran her finger over her pendant and focused on taking slow, calming breaths, willing her frazzled thoughts to settle. She felt the truth of Fiona's guidance. Demanding answers immediately would only lead her astray. The path would show the way when she was ready.

Opening her eyes, she managed a tremulous smile. "You're right. I can't force this. But please, if you sense anything that could help..."

Fiona patted her hand reassuringly. "You have a unique gift and a kind soul. I have faith that your purpose and skills will grow." She tilted her head, considering Shelby thoughtfully. "In the meantime, you may find additional allies to guide your way. Let them help. And remember that when your mind is twirling and racing, it's impossible to use your skills to their full potential. Practice calm, even in chaotic situations. A calm mind creates a powerful mind, and a powerful mind creates powerful skills."

Harper trilled her approval.

Shelby nodded, feeling less alone in her bewildering predicament. If wise Fiona believed help would come, she would try to be patient and watchful for those meant to join her.

"There are many people in town who care about Mr. Peacock," Fiona pointed out. "You're not alone in your desire to help him."

After a few more moments of companionable silence, Shelby nodded, set down her emptied teacup, and stood reluctantly. "Thank you for your guidance. I know I need to let all of this unfold in its own way and time."

Fiona walked her to the curtained doorway with Harper trailing behind them. "Keep hope, dear one. The clouds will part to reveal the sun."

Stepping back out into the deepening winter dusk, Shelby felt her earlier panic turn into a quiet determination. Answers waited in the shadows. She would move forward cautiously, trusting her senses to light the path as she navigated this strange new world.

Harper glanced at Shelby as they headed home. "Take heart. You have good friends," the cat told her.

Shelby smiled and reached down to stroke the cat's silky fur.

Nearing the Spellbound Bookshop, she was surprised to see Lucy about to enter the shop with a bakery box in hand. Shelby quickened her pace, waving when her friend glanced up.

"Hey! I was hoping I'd catch you," Lucy said, holding the door open. A rush of cozy warmth enveloped the two friends as they stepped inside. "I come bearing sugary sustenance."

Soon the two were tucked side-by-side on the sofa near the fireplace, mugs of cocoa and a plate of pastries on the coffee table before them. Shelby closed her eyes blissfully as she bit into a flaky croissant, the buttery layers melting on her tongue.

Lucy grinned at her obvious enjoyment. "I thought you could use a pick-me-up with everything that's going on. Oh, and I brought some catnip cookies for Harper, too," she added, tossing one to the waiting feline.

Shelby smiled gratefully at her thoughtful friend. Lucy's happy spirit never failed to lift her own. "Thank you. This is just what I needed."

As they ate, Shelby confided her frustration at being unable to tap into her psychic senses to help Mr. Peacock. Lucy listened, absently stroking Harper where the cat was curled up between them.

"Fiona gave you good advice. Be patient with

yourself," Lucy advised gently when Shelby had finished venting. "From what I've seen, your abilities are growing stronger. This is all new to you. It's just a matter of time before things click into place."

Lucy gave her friend an encouraging nudge with her shoulder. "For now, do what you can and trust it's enough. You've got this."

Shelby's eyes misted at her friend's unwavering faith. However confusing her path was, Lucy's support would help her move forward. "Thanks for being my friend."

After warm hugs and making plans to meet tomorrow, Lucy headed home, and Shelby moved slowly about the shadowy shop tidying up. Despite lingering worries, the familiar space calmed her. She paused to trail her fingers over the spines of the books lining the shelves - each one a way to discover knew things and lift the spirit.

With a small, determined smile, Shelby flipped the sign on the front entrance to "Closed." Answers about the crime waited somewhere in the dark – and she would try to help find them, one step at a time. She headed upstairs to her cozy apartment with Harper padding ahead of her on the landing.

It was time to rest.

10

Shelby glanced up from sorting a box of new releases as the bell above the bookshop door announced a new arrival. She blinked in surprise as Detective Whitely strode in looking imposing in his long black, wool coat.

"Detective Whitely," she greeted him cautiously. Whatever news had brought him to the bookshop, she was afraid it wouldn't be anything good.

The man gave her a faint smile as he approached the counter. "Please, call me Travis. No need to be formal."

"Right, okay ... Travis." Shelby hoped her cheeks weren't as pink as they felt under his intent gaze. His informal request reminded her how little she really knew the man behind the badge.

An awkward pause stretched before Travis broke it, clearing his throat. "I have an update on the case I thought you should know about. We got an ID back on the male victim."

Shelby perked up, thoughts instantly refocusing. "You found out who the man at the estate was?"

Travis nodded. "His name was Allen Jones, a petty criminal known to the police in both Silver Cove and Sweet Cove. He had a history of burglaries and theft in those towns. I guess he was spreading his net a little wider and decided to try the town of Hamlet."

He watched Shelby closely as he continued. "It seems Jones broke into two other homes in Hamlet the same night he hit up Peacock's place. It was the wrong house at the wrong time, unfortunately for him."

Shelby absorbed the news, her mind churning. "So, this Jones fellow accidentally stumbled onto the killer lying in wait for Peacock." She shivered, once again imagining the tragic sequence of events.

"That's our working theory," Travis confirmed. "Since Jones was in Mr. Peacock's home and had Peacock's wallet on him when he died, the murderer clearly mistook him for the intended target."

Pacing behind the counter, Shelby struggled to

fit this new information into the puzzle. "Do you think Jones and the killer might have known each other? Were they robbing people's homes together? But if Jones was just a petty thief, I suppose he wouldn't work with a partner." Her brow furrowed in thought. "If the killer murdered the thief thinking it was Mr. Peacock, why would he dump the body at the Harris Estate? And why light the fire afterward?"

Travis spread his hands. "Your guess is as good as mine. Another of our theories is that after murdering the thief, the killer realized his mistake and decided to remove the body from the home so as not to tip off the police or Mr. Peacock. We're also looking into any connection between Jones and Peacock's legal career that might explain why Jones decided to rob that house, but I don't think there's a connection between Jones and Peacock. I believe the *killer* has a link to Peacock. As for the fire..." He frowned. "Once he realized his mistake, it seems the fire was meant to obscure the victim's identity."

Shelby's shoulders slumped. She'd hoped learning the victim's identity would bring clarity, but instead, more questions cluttered her mind.

Noticing her dejected expression, Travis stepped closer and lowered his voice. "I know it's frustrating, but we're making progress. And..." He hesitated before continuing. "Your insights could still help, if you're open to it."

Shelby looked up, startled by the offer. Travis held her gaze earnestly. "I can tell you have an ability to see what others miss. We could use that." He smiled slightly. "Think about it?"

Heart fluttered again, and Shelby managed a shy nod. Travis's belief in her abilities meant more than she could say. She wanted nothing more than to use her skills to keep people safe.

"I will. Thank you for updating me ... and for your trust." She hoped he understood the depth of her gratitude.

With a final meaningful look, Travis donned his winter hat and headed out into the deepening winter twilight. Shelby remained motionless behind the counter long after he had gone, her pulse still racing and her cheeks still warm.

Finally rousing herself, she set about closing up the shop for the evening, moving distractedly through the routine tasks. Her thoughts revolved around the scant new clues, trying to figure out any connections.

What linked a murdered petty thief to the esteemed James Peacock, besides proximity and cruel fate? She feared the answer involved secrets that placed the kindly gentleman in mortal danger.

At the thought of Peacock, Shelby froze. How secure was he, alone each night with only routine police patrols as protection? Was there something she could do to help? But what could she realistically do?

No, working with Travis to uncover the truth was her only real option. However unsettled Shelby still felt by her emerging psychic talents, she had to try and master them enough to find the killer before he could strike again.

Closing up the shop in a pensive mood, Shelby climbed the stairs to her cozy apartment. The savory aroma of homemade soup greeted her as she unlocked the door.

Lucy stood at the stove stirring a large pot, while Harper watched intently from her perch atop the nearby counter. They both glanced up with matching expressions as Shelby entered.

"There you are. Your dinner awaits," Lucy pronounced with an exaggerated bow. "I texted you that I was going to your apartment to make soup, but you didn't answer."

Despite her grim thoughts, Shelby had to smile.

Trust Lucy to appear with comfort food and friendship right when she needed it most.

Soon the two were seated at the little kitchen table with heaping bowls of chunky vegetable soup and a fresh baguette. Shelby savored the delicious food.

Later, sitting together on the plush sofa, Shelby confided the new details Travis had shared. Lucy listened thoughtfully, absently stroking Harper where she was curled up in a purring ball next to her.

"So Jones broke into the house by chance and stole Peacock's wallet ... and the killer assumed he was the correct target," Lucy mused aloud. She shook her head. "Talk about being in the worst place at the worst time."

Shelby shivered. "I know Travis must be doing everything he can, but I hate feeling powerless to stop all of this. Mr. Peacock shouldn't have to live in fear."

Lucy squeezed her hand. "Your skills are growing every day and Travis clearly has faith in you," she added with a sly smile. "You two will crack this case. I know you will."

Buoyed by her friend's confidence, Shelby

managed a small smile. For now, she just had to trust the steady development of her talents.

Later, curled up in bed with Harper's soothing presence near her feet, Shelby's thoughts drifted back to Travis. She could see the compassion behind his reserved exterior when he spoke of protecting the vulnerable.

She drifted off with his parting words echoing through her mind ... "Think about it."

Oh, she sure would. About several things. She couldn't get Travis out of her head.

The next evening, Shelby carefully balanced a covered basket as she made her way up the snow-dusted walkway to Mr. Peacock's charming cottage with Harper padding along with her. She had baked fresh blueberry muffins that morning, hoping the muffins might lift the man's spirits after the recent distress.

Shelby rapped gently on the bright red door, and Mr. Peacock opened it a moment later. His face broke into a pleased grin at the sight of the pair on his doorstep.

"Shelby, my dear. And clever Harper too.

Welcome, please come in." He stepped aside so they could enter the cozy warmth of his home.

Soon Shelby and Mr. Peacock were settled at the kitchen table with steaming mugs of Earl Grey tea and a plate of warm muffins between them. Harper made herself right at home on the man's lap, purring loudly as he stroked her glossy fur.

Shelby's heart swelled at seeing the contented smile creasing the man's kind face. She was relieved the recent turmoil hadn't dampened his cheerful spirit.

"How have you been holding up?" she asked gently after he had complimented her baking skills. "I know it's been an impossibly stressful time."

Mr. Peacock sighed, though his eyes still had their twinkle. "Oh, plodding along well enough. Being back at the library today helped take my mind off worried thoughts. And I had an alarm system installed yesterday which makes this old place feel a whole lot safer."

He took a sip of tea before adding, "I've been trying not to dwell on all of it, though it still baffles me completely. I have no idea who would do such a dreadful thing."

Shelby stirred honey into her tea, considering how to delicately broach her real reason for visiting.

She didn't want to cause more distress, but details could be key to stopping the threat.

"I wondered if in looking back over your legal career, any specific cases came to mind? Maybe some people who might have harbored some deep resentment even years later?"

Mr. Peacock sat back with his brow furrowed in concentration. "The police asked me the same thing. As a prosecutor, I put away some unsavory characters who seemed the vengeful type, but I believe they're all still securely incarcerated."

He shook his head regretfully. "If it is someone with an old grudge, I'm afraid I have no idea who it could be. We locked up many dangerous individuals. I always tried to do right in my prosecutions, but not all felt justice was served."

Gazing into the fire crackling merrily in the small kitchen hearth, Mr. Peacock's expression turned wistful. "I do wish Cecelia were still here with me, but I wouldn't want her caught up in this mess. I miss her every day."

Shelby made a sympathetic sound, recalling that Mr. Peacock's beloved wife had passed away a few years ago after a long and happy marriage.

He gave her a kind smile, patting Harper soothingly. "We often forget to cherish our loved ones in the busyness of life, but staring mortality in the face reminds you how precious those connections are. I thank heavens that our son is safe in Texas."

He shook his head as if to clear away his thoughts. "But listen to me prattling on with gloomy philosophizing. I'm grateful that you came by. I hope the police can quickly find the one responsible for all this trouble. I feel very bad for the man who was killed."

As Harper stood up on the man's lap and licked his cheek, Shelby's throat tightened with emotion. Even under threat, Mr. Peacock's thoughts turned to others. She was humbled by his kind spirit.

They passed the rest of the visit chatting about lighter topics until Shelby noticed the clock showed it was nearing ten. "I should let you get some rest," she said reluctantly, standing and gathering her things.

Mr. Peacock walked her to the door with Harper winding around their legs. "Thank you for the thoughtful company, my dear. It does a person good to have compassionate people like you and your wonderful Harper looking after him."

He drew Shelby into a paternal hug. "This cloud will pass," he whispered. "Keep your heart light."

Blinking back sudden tears, Shelby squeezed his

hand warmly. She hoped he was right and the police would soon find the perpetrator.

Strolling home through the peaceful night with Harper trotting loyally at her side, Shelby was determined to hold onto the hope and wisdom Mr. Peacock modeled and, if she could, help Travis find the killer.

Glancing up at the full moon, Shelby let its glow soothe her worries.

She drew the cold, crisp night air deep into her lungs, letting it push away the cobwebs of fear and doubt. For now.

11

The next morning, Shelby ran next door to the café for a quick cup of takeout coffee. While standing in line, she waved at Chad the barista who was busy steaming milk and preparing lattes for the morning rush of customers. The cozy café was filled with people chatting and the rich aroma of freshly brewed coffee.

A moment later, Shelby heard a voice call her name and she turned around to see a college friend coming up to her.

"Courtney!" A wide smile spread over Shelby's face. "What are you doing here?"

Courtney Roseland lived about thirty minutes away in the seaside town of Sweet Cove where she was the co-owner of a charming candy shop and an art gallery on the main street of town. Shelby hadn't seen her friend for some time.

Courtney's honey-blonde hair bounced over her shoulders as she hurried over, her pretty face lighting up when she saw Shelby.

Shelby and Courtney hugged one another, and when they did, each of them felt a surprising zip of electrical energy run between them. When they stepped back, they stared at each other for a few seconds not quite understanding what had just happened.

"Angie and I took the train up to do some holiday shopping." Courtney gestured to her sister who was purchasing coffee and pastries at the counter.

"Hey, Shelby. Nice to see you," Angie said with a friendly smile, her shoulder-length hair shining under the café lights. "We were planning to go to your bookshop right after lunch."

"Nice to see you, too, Angie. You both look great." Shelby smiled, taking in her friends' stylish outfits and easy-going manner. She'd always enjoyed being with the sisters.

"Can you sit for a bit with us?" Courtney asked.

"I shouldn't, but I'd like to catch up."

The three women took their coffees and pastries to a table that opened up by the windows where the winter morning sunlight filtered in, glinting off the polished wood surfaces.

"We heard about the fire and the murder," Courtney told her friend. "Bad stuff."

Shelby frowned. "A case of mistaken identity. The killer was really after a retired man from town who now works at the library part-time and writes crime fiction. He used to work as a lawyer. He's a very nice man and everyone in town likes him." She leaned a little closer. "So, it sort of makes it feel like an attack on all of us."

"We understand," Angie said. "Sweet Cove is a small town, too, and we try to take care of each other when something goes wrong."

"I know you help the police," Shelby said. "How did you get into that?"

"Our grandmother used to help the police with some cases." Courtney took a sip from her cup. "She had very strong analytical skills." She left out the part that their grandmother had paranormal skills that came in handy when trying to help solve a case.

"When we all moved to Sweet Cove, the police chief approached us and asked if we wanted to help out on occasion with some cases like our grandmother used to do," Angie explained.

Angie also left out the fact that she and her four sisters had inherited some paranormal skills from their mother and grandmother who were descended from a long line of psychics and intuits. The Sweet Cove chief of police knew about the family's special skills, and that was the reason he'd invited them to consult on some cases.

Courtney had never told Shelby about their family abilities. "Is there anything new on the case?" she asked.

"The police identified the man who was killed in error," Shelby told the young women. "He was a petty thief. He had committed a number of burglaries in your town. He was known to the police." She went on to fill them in on the burglar's criminal background. "I guess he decided to try robbing people here in Hamlet. Before he was killed in James Peacock's house, he had broken into two other houses in town."

"He sure was in the wrong place at the wrong time," Angie noted.

Courtney said, "The police must have assigned protection to Mr. Peacock?"

"Not really." Shelby sighed. "They don't have the

resources to protect the man 24/7. Mr. Peacock did have a security system installed though."

"That's a good thing." Courtney nodded, looking thoughtful. She and Angie shared a subtle glance that made Shelby wonder if they knew more than they were letting on about the case, but the moment passed quickly. "How is Mr. Peacock holding up?"

"Worried, but not paralyzed with fear. He still goes to work at the library and sees friends," Shelby told them.

Courtney's eyes widened. "I'm not sure I'd handle it so well if someone were coming after me."

"I feel the same way," Shelby admitted. "I wish there was some way I could help the police."

"You could ask them if there was something you could volunteer to help with," Angie said. "The police are often shorthanded. They might jump at the chance to have you help out."

"The detective on the case told me I had strong intuition and that I noticed things others overlook." Shelby blushed a little.

Courtney narrowed her eyes. "Is he cute?"

Shelby's cheeks went full-blown red. "He's not bad to look at."

The young women chuckled.

"Then maybe you should ask that detective if

there was some way you could be of service." Courtney smiled and raised an eyebrow, and the other two laughed.

When Courtney reached for one of the napkins on the table, her hand brushed against Shelby's and she felt the same electrical zip she'd felt when they'd hugged. Courtney stared at her friend, and she knew Shelby had felt the same sensation. "Is there anything new with you?"

Shelby looked down at her coffee cup. "Nothing, really. Just working, hanging out with friends, hiking, and seeing my family."

Angie asked how Shelby's family was doing.

"Everyone's good. My parents are both working and taking care of their animals. My brother is still working as a financial planner in the next town over."

"How's the bookshop doing?" Courtney asked.

"Great. I couldn't ask for more. Running my own place is a dream come true."

"And how's Harper?"

Shelby chuckled. "The same as always. Bossing me around and sucking up to the bookshop customers."

"She's a special cat," Courtney observed.

Shelby made eye contact with her friend for a

moment. It almost seemed like Courtney knew what happened after she'd fallen off the ladder. "I fell off a ladder the other day."

"Did you?" Angie asked. "You weren't hurt?"

"No. I was trying to hang a holiday wreath over the fireplace when I slipped on a rung and went tumbling backward. I got a huge egg on the back of my head, and I think I passed out for a few seconds, but that was all."

"Did you get checked out by a doctor?"

"No, I didn't have any signs of a concussion or anything like that," Shelby told them.

Courtney studied the young woman's face. "No lasting effects of any kind?"

Shelby looked away. She felt as if her friend sensed something was different about her. "Not really."

"Well, see a doctor if anything changes," Courtney suggested.

"I will." Shelby checked the time and regretfully slid her chair back. "I should get back to the shop."

"Are you free for lunch?" Angie asked. "Want to join us?"

Shelby shook her head. "I can't get away for lunch. What about dinner? Will you still be in town then?"

"We're heading back on the 4 pm train," Courtney said. "This trip was a spur of the moment thing. Next time, we'll have to plan better so we can spend more time together."

"I'd like that."

The women walked to the door together and when they were out on the sidewalk, Shelby and Courtney hugged again holding on a beat longer as that intriguing energy hummed between them once again. Then Shelby hugged Angie before hurrying back to the bookshop. Ducking inside into the warmth of her shop, Shelby leaned against the door for a moment to catch her breath. The encounter with her old friends had left her unsettled in a way she didn't quite understand. Shaking it off, she hung up her coat and went back to work.

When Shelby was out of ear shot, Courtney turned to her sister. "Did you feel that?"

"Yup." Angie raised an eyebrow.

"Something's up with her." Courtney watched Shelby go into her bookstore. "It seems like she's developing powers ... maybe from that fall she took. I never felt it from her when we were in college."

"When you were in college, you didn't know *you* had powers," Angie pointed out with a smile.

"True. I'd like to talk to her, but if I'm wrong about her, I'm afraid she might think I'm nuts."

"Ah, the eternal problem when people have secrets they need to keep hidden." Angie slipped her hand through her sister's arm and they started walking up Main Street to do some more shopping.

12

Shelby looked around at the elegantly decorated venue, smiling as she took in the twinkling lights, fragrant garlands, vases of roses and greens on the tables, an ice sculpture, and the polished wood dance floor. The annual holiday party to benefit the historical society never failed to impress. This year they'd rented a ballroom in a fancy hotel that usually catered to weddings, and the room had been transformed into a magical wonderland.

Crystal chandeliers cast a soft glow over the formally attired guests chatting and sipping cocktails, and the tables set for dinner gleamed with fine China, silverware, crystal goblets, and candles. An orchestra played softly on a small stage, setting a festive mood.

Shelby turned to Lucy, who was similarly awed by the lavish atmosphere. "Can you believe how gorgeous they made this place look? I'm glad I bought a new dress."

Ross Billings, Lucy's casual boyfriend said, "This place looks fantastic." Ross's father and mother owned the inn where Lucy was employed as the baker.

Lucy grinned at her friend. "I love your dress. You look beautiful. And being here gives us a chance to mingle with some of Hamlet's well-connected citizens." The young woman nodded discreetly toward a group of well-dressed men and women who Shelby recognized as important business owners and town officials.

Self-consciously, Shelby smoothed non-existent wrinkles from her dark green velvet dress. Lucy was right - tonight provided access to influential people who might have insights to help the investigation.

As the friends threaded their way through the growing crowd exchanging holiday greetings, Shelby's nerves began to fade. Despite the formal setting, the atmosphere remained relaxed and jovial and was filled with familiar faces.

Her gaze was drawn to a tall man standing

ramrod straight near the orchestra. Detective Travis Whitely cut an impressive figure in a crisp black suit.

Shelby realized she was staring and quickly shifted her focus, hoping no one had noticed, but when she glanced back a moment later, Travis's dark eyes were watching her through the crowd.

Her face warming, she deliberately turned away to study a display of antique photographs and paintings of the town hanging along one wall. She could almost feel the weight of Travis's gaze still lingering on her back. Strange, unsettled excitement simmered in her veins.

"Oh good, here's Patrice and her husband," Lucy said.

Shelby turned with a genuine smile as their friends approached.

"You both look so nice," Shelby told the older couple warmly.

Patrice smiled, patting her husband Ron's arm.

"I wanted to dress up. It's so nice to have an occasion to wear a pretty dress." Her bright tone faltered slightly. "We nearly didn't attend, after ... everything that's gone on. But I convinced Ron that staying home would feel too much like giving in to fear."

Shelby nodded somberly, not needing to ask

what the woman meant. The shadow cast by Mr. Peacock's close call still lingered for all of them.

As if hearing her thoughts, a familiar lanky figure appeared at Patrice's side. "Good evening, ladies!" Mr. Peacock greeted them jovially. "Don't the decorations look wonderful?"

Despite the heavy security in place, seeing the gentleman out and about set Shelby's mind at ease. Mr. Peacock seemed determined not to hide away from community life, staring down fear with resilience. Shelby admired his courage.

"It's nice to see you." She squeezed the man's hand. "We weren't sure if you'd come."

"I wouldn't miss it." Peacock leaned closer. "I'm probably safer in a big group of people than I am sitting in my house alone."

"Well, I'm glad to see you." Shelby smiled.

"The historical society president asked me to give a short reading from my most recent book about the history of Hamlet." Mr. Peacock chuckled. "I agreed to share a brief bit of history about the town. Hopefully, I won't put everyone straight to sleep." His eyes twinkled merrily behind his spectacles.

"I'm sure it will be very interesting," Lucy told him.

"I'm looking forward to it," Ross told the man.

The chatter lulled as the president of the historical society took the stage to welcome them. As introductions and acknowledgments droned on, Shelby's gaze was once more drawn magnetically across the room to where Travis stood listening intently.

When the speech ended, the lights dimmed further and music swelled as couples drifted onto the dancefloor. Shelby was content to watch the twirling guests from her seat at their table, sneaking glances at Travis moving gracefully with an elegant older woman she thought might be his mother.

"Would you care to dance, my dear?" Mr. Peacock appeared at her side, gallantly extending a hand. Beaming, Shelby let him lead her into the swaying crowd.

Her eyes shone brightly as they spun across the polished floor to the upbeat orchestra music. Mr. Peacock expertly guided them through intricate steps before walking her back to the table where he executed an exaggerated bow that made Shelby laugh out loud.

After dancing a lively fox trot with Ron, Patrice joined Lucy and Shelby in a quiet nook near the bar to chat and catch her breath. Shelby sipped champagne, enjoying the celebratory mood and the chance to speak casually with the townsfolk in attendance.

When the mayor wandered over to discuss a potential book signing at Spellbound Books by a local author, Lucy and Patrice went back to the table. Once the mayor finished talking to her, Shelby noticed Travis standing several yards away looking like he was at loose ends now that the dancing had ended.

When her heart fluttered, Shelby reminded herself he was simply a professional contact who she was occasionally assisting with an investigation, but she couldn't tear her eyes away from his striking profile, appreciating how the formal wear highlighted his athletic frame.

Steeling her courage, she stepped closer. "Hello, Detective."

The man turned, eyebrows lifting in that subtly amused way she was coming to know. "I thought we agreed you'd call me Travis." His smile made her glad she'd approached.

"Oh, right, I just wasn't sure..." Shelby trailed off, feeling suddenly shy.

He looked at her intently and she hoped the low lighting hid her flushed cheeks.

"You look really nice," he said simply. Before she

could come up with an intelligible response, he added lightly, "Are you enjoying the party?"

Shelby released a shaky exhale. Soon they were chatting comfortably about holiday traditions and favorite seasonal foods. She found Travis surprisingly easy to talk to when she could tamp down her distracting awareness of his nearness.

Across the room, Lucy caught her eye and gave an enthusiastic thumbs up. Mortified, Shelby angled herself to block Travis's view but suspected he had noticed her friend's antics when she saw his little smile.

Thankfully, he didn't say anything about it. Instead he nodded to where Mr. Peacock stood preparing to give his reading. "Should we take our seats to listen?"

He walked with Shelby to her table, and then went to sit with his companions. As Mr. Peacock was being introduced, she leaned over to whisper to Lucy, "I'll get back at you for embarrassing me in front of Travis. Just you wait."

Looking gleeful, her friend just grinned before turning an innocent gaze on Shelby. "What do you mean? I'm just happy to see you enjoying yourself."

Shelby huffed, but a small smile slipped over her lips as she settled in to listen to the excerpt Mr.

Peacock had chosen to read from his most recent historical book. His pleasant voice transported them into the past, bringing characters and details to life.

Too soon, he was closing the book's cover to enthusiastic applause. Shelby clapped eagerly as the man returned to their table where he gave a little seated bow of acknowledgment that made her laugh.

As dinner was served, Mr. Peacock regaled the people at the table with theatrical reenactments from his speaking days in courtrooms. Shelby threw back her head, laughing until tears prickled when he impersonated a pompous judge.

It showed the man's many qualities - keenly insightful, whimsical, and quick-witted. Shelby hoped the case would be solved soon so the shadow of worry hanging over him would pass.

Over dessert, she leaned forward to ask Mr. Peacock a question that had been on her mind lately. "Did you know much about the history of the Spellbound Books building before I took ownership? I've been trying to research more on the building's past."

Mr. Peacock launched eagerly into lecture mode, delighted by the subject. "Why yes, as a matter of fact. The building was built in 1805 and a young woman named Emily Harris ran a shop there. I understand Emily was quite the business pioneer for her time."

He lowered his voice conspiratorially. "Now, this next part is mere rumor, but intriguing nonetheless." After a moment, he continued, "Word was, Emily had amassed quite a valuable stamp collection from her worldwide correspondence for the bookshop. A man desperate to obtain the collection pursued her tirelessly, certain she was hiding rare finds."

Mr. Peacock shook his head regretfully. "When Emily refused to sell to this aggressive fellow, he resorted to violence to seize the stamps. One night he broke in and attacked the poor woman. She perished from her injuries."

Shelby shivered at the chilling tale. A dangerous obsession had cut short an innocent life. She made a mental note to research public records for more on Emily's tragic end.

The band struck up a lively tune that drew couples back to the dance floor before Shelby could ask anything further. Watching the swirling dresses and graceful steps, she found herself wishing she could dance with Travis, but then shook her head at such a silly idea. Their relationship was all business.

The evening wound toward a close with more dancing and socializing. Shelby left the party after extracting Lucy and Ross from an increasingly tipsy group of revelers near the bar. She was quiet and thoughtful during the ride home.

Later tossing restlessly in bed, thoughts of Emily Harris's violent demise at the hands of a killer refused to let go of her mind. Had the man simply wanted the stamp collection or was there something more behind the murder? Was he angry at Emily for some reason? Was he jealous that a woman owned her own shop? Had they not gotten along? Maybe the killer had fallen in love with the young woman, but she didn't share his feelings and rebuffed him.

With a frustrated sigh, Shelby turned her pillow over and closed her eyes willing herself to fall asleep.

13

Shelby sank onto the overstuffed armchair with a contented sigh, savoring the cozy quiet of her apartment. Gentle snowflakes drifted past the frost-lined windows as evening darkness covered the sleepy town. It was a perfect night to be inside, safe and warm.

Harper leapt lightly onto Shelby's lap, settling into a purring ball. Absently stroking the sleek fur, Shelby let her thoughts roam over the eventful days since her world had tilted on its axis. So much had changed. She hardly recognized herself and who she was becoming - open to things beyond ordinary perception, her senses were expanding in ways both frightening and exciting.

Yet for all the upheaval, the upstairs apartment

was still her sanctuary. Shelby smiled softly, gazing around at the cherished books piled on the side tables and on the bookshelves lining the walls, the trailing ivy she'd rescued from neglect, and the quilt draped over the sofa that her grandmother had stitched.

The cozy apartment above the shop had felt like home the moment she'd walked into it, but now she understood she shared the dwelling with a kindred spirit who loved it just as much - the gentle ghost Emily, who in life had filled the shop with her hopes and dreams.

Emily didn't reveal herself often. The ghost seemed content to dwell peacefully in the shadows of the shop full of her memories. Instead of being unnerved by the presence of the spirit, Shelby thought of the ghost as a watchful guardian.

"Harper, you've spoken with our resident ghost?" Shelby asked on impulse. The cat's wide green eyes blinked up at her.

"On occasion. I'm aware of her energy. Emily means no harm; she just wants to stay close to the place she loved in life."

Shelby nodded slowly, looking off across the room at nothing. "Emily met a violent end, murdered by someone who wanted what was hers."

She refocused her attention back on Harper. "Do you know anything about what happened to her?"

The cat's plumed tail flicked thoughtfully. "She's private about her murder and hesitant to revisit such pain. But if she ever wants to share her story, I'll listen to the terrible tale."

Shelby reached over to scratch Harper's chin. "I'd like to talk to her about her life. Of course, Emily deserves compassion and distance from the awful death she experienced." Her instincts told her the long-ago crime that cut Emily's future short could hold meaning for the present troubles in Hamlet. "I wonder if Emily could help us find some clues about the person who wants to hurt Mr. Peacock. I wonder if she could help point to a suspect." Shelby knew she couldn't push the ghost to interact with her. She had to treat the spirit with kindness and patience.

She stood and moved to the too-full bookshelf lining one wall. After a few minutes scanning the haphazard titles, she pulled down a thin, leather-bound volume - a genealogy of Hamlet's founding families commissioned by the historical society in the 1970s.

Flipping carefully through the pages, Shelby soon found the entry for Emily Harris, born in 1890 to parents George and Catherine. Catherine came from a family of prosperous merchants and was the sole heir to significant assets and George ran a shop for men's and women's clothing and accessories on the main street of town. They welcomed their daughter Emily late in life.

Skimming the details of Emily's early years, Shelby pieced together a picture of a sheltered but willful only child. Catherine succumbed to fever when Emily was fourteen, leaving her alone with her devoted father. By all accounts, it had been an idyllic upbringing filled with music, books, and some travel. Emily had a good mind for business and helped her father with the shops and land investments.

Things changed abruptly when George also passed unexpectedly from heart failure just after Emily's twenty-first birthday. Inheriting her mother's fortune, Emily became one of the wealthiest young women in town - and suddenly completely independent.

Rather than sell the small shop George had built, Emily invested in expanding it into a two-story building and she added books and gifts to the shop's inventory. In an age when women rarely participated in business, Emily defiantly took charge, personally corresponding with book dealers and merchants to stock the shelves of the store.

Under her careful stewardship, the store thrived, but Emily remained unmarried, refusing several eligible local suitors. Although she always worried that men were only interested in her because of her money, Emily appeared to have been content in her self-sufficient life surrounded by friends and community ... until her tragic end at just twenty-six-years old.

Shelby closed the genealogy softly. Reading the book, she'd glimpsed flashes of the spirited woman Emily had been - intelligent, creative, yearning for meaning and connection, and protective of her autonomy.

Laying a hand gently on the book's cover, Shelby whispered, "I hope you found some happiness here pursuing your life's interests."

Rousing herself from the melancholy musings, she shelved the volume and headed downstairs to the bookshop with Harper padding behind her. Shelby left the lights off, moving confidently through the darkness of her store, and sat on the comfortable sofa. She patted the cushion next to her in invitation, and Harper jumped up and circled twice before settling with her chin resting lightly atop Shelby's knee.

Closing her eyes, Shelby focused on taking deep even breaths, allowing her *sensitivity* to expand and unfold like a flower turning toward the sun. Under Fiona's watchful guidance, she had been practicing sending her energy out into the world. Anchored by Harper's solid presence, Shelby tried to send her thoughts drifting through the still air.

Emily? Please don't be afraid of me. I'd like to talk to you.

Silence.

"She won't talk to you directly," Harper explained. "Ask her to tell me her words so I can relay them to you."

"Emily, could you tell Harper what you'd like to say to me? Then Harper can speak to my mind."

A nearly imperceptible whisper brushed by Shelby.

Harper nodded. "She says some stories are too painful to be retold. Let the dead keep their secrets."

Shelby shivered as goosebumps rippled down her arms and pressed on tenderly but persistently to communicate with the ghost.

"You endured something terrible, but you don't

have to carry it alone. We only want to help you cross over ... to be free, if that's what you wish to do."

Something vibrated through the atmosphere, like particles of energy swirling in agitation. When Emily's strained reply came, Shelby had to fight not to recoil from the awful sadness in what she said.

Harper said, "This is Emily's reply ... Free? This place alone is my freedom. Why resurrect the horror I cannot outrun, even in death? Please, leave the past in the past. My soul is too scarred by cruel hands. Leave my body in its grave and allow my spirit to remain here in this place."

As the faint presence receded, Shelby closed her eyes for a moment as her emotions churned. She would respect Emily's wishes. She wouldn't encourage the spirit to cross over, but she wanted to be friends with the ghost. She would have to take her time. She would have to win Emily's trust.

"You're welcome to remain here in the Spellbound Bookshop for as long as you like." Shelby stroked Harper's back. "Thanks for helping me communicate with Emily," she told the cat.

The next morning, Shelby felt exhausted and mechanically went through the motions of getting ready for the day. A fresh dusting of snow glittered under the rising sun, erasing all tracks and frozen slush into a clean blanket of white.

A knock on her apartment door announced Lucy's arrival and tugged Shelby from her thoughts. She mustered a smile for her friend who came inside carrying a grocery bag.

"I thought I'd take a detour over here before I head to the inn. I brought supplies for a nice breakfast," Lucy explained, already unpacking eggs and bread onto the kitchen counter. "You look like you could use some comfort food and girl talk."

Soon cinnamon-spiced oatmeal with generous drizzles of maple syrup lifted Shelby's spirits. Seated across from Lucy, she recounted her strange interaction with Emily the night before.

Her friend listened thoughtfully, petting Harper on her lap. "That's tough." Lucy blew out a sigh once Shelby had finished explaining her dilemma. "You want to help Emily, but not at the cost of retraumatizing her."

She considered the problem, her forehead crinkling. "Maybe there's a way to uncover some information without forcing Emily to confront her pain. Maybe you can find some facts from other sources?"

Shelby nodded slowly. Lucy's solution allowed her to keep digging while honoring Emily's need for distance. "You're right. Maybe just learning the murderer's motive could bring some small measure of closure for her."

She smiled at her friend. "Have I mentioned lately how lost I'd be without your insights to balance out my bullheadedness?"

Lucy waved off the praise, but her smile grew wide. "You'd have figured it out. I just want to see that poor ghost find peace." Her expression turned uncharacteristically somber. "And make sure history doesn't repeat itself."

Shelby nodded in understanding. "I know I have to respect the ghost's wishes, but it seems so wrong for her to linger when she could cross over and be in a better place. She's stuck here. I think if she crossed, she could find peace and happiness again."

"Maybe she just needs time." Lucy checked her watch. "We'd better get to work."

"Thanks for the delicious breakfast." Shelby rose to begin another day.

Hours later as dusk settled over the town, the shop bell's merry jingle announced Fiona slipping in with a swirl of her patchouli-scented shawl. Shelby greeted her mentor warmly.

"Tea?" Shelby offered, already moving toward the kettle while Fiona settled gracefully on the plush sofa near the fireplace, nodding with a small smile.

Soon Shelby joined her with two steaming cups. Inhaling the earthy aromas of herbs and flowers usually centered her scattered thoughts, but today her mind couldn't settle.

Fiona seemed content not to force conversation, allowing the quiet between them to work its magic, but her keen gaze assessed the younger woman over the rim of her teacup.

"Your spirit is uneasy," the psychic remarked after several more minutes of silence. "Tell me what burdens you."

Haltingly, Shelby confessed to wanting to investigate Emily's murder to see if she could find the reason the ghost wouldn't cross into the next world. She explained that Emily didn't seem to want anyone to help her cross. She wanted to stay where she was.

Fiona listened, her brow furrowing as Shelby explained her reluctance to cause more harm to Emily's soul.

When she concluded, Fiona set down her empty

cup with care. "You have a kind heart, not wanting to distress her," the woman said gently. "Yet looking into the murder won't harm her as long as you don't share the details with the spirit. Find out what you can, then decide if telling Emily will help or hurt her."

Fiona held Shelby's gaze. "In the end, we can't protect anyone from their pains. What matters is how we walk with them through their troubles toward healing. Be Emily's compassionate witness, and let the rest unfold as it must."

Shelby released a slow breath, feeling that Fiona was right.

"You already sense the way forward." Fiona rose gracefully. "Have faith in your gifts, and you'll do the right thing."

Shelby walked her friend and mentor to the door with a lighter heart. The falling snow had stopped, leaving the street pristine and peaceful in the deepening winter twilight. Shelby tipped her face up to admire the emerging stars and then waved farewell to Fiona as the woman disappeared down the lamp-lit sidewalk.

When she turned to go back inside, a hint of a shadow at the corner of the side street made her pause, but in the blink of an eye, whatever it was,

was gone, leaving Shelby to wonder if she had imagined the silhouette that seemed to be watching her.

With a shiver, she quickly slipped into the warmth of the shop, flipped the sign to "Closed," and locked the door.

14

A festive atmosphere filled Spellbound Books as customers mingled through the cozy space browsing discounted titles, sipping warm beverages, and eating sweets. Twinkling lights and greenery adorned the front counter where an array of baked treats tempted hungry shoppers. Near the fireplace, Patrice and Ron Nelson managed a beverage station, cheerfully doling out steaming mugs of coffee and hot cocoa.

Shelby paused to admire the cheerful scene. She had organized this holiday "Sips, Sweets, and Shop Sale" event to thank the community for its support this past year. Judging by the lively crowd packing the store, her bookshop idea had been a success.

Weaving through the throng with a tray of gingerbread men, Shelby smiled as she caught snippets of conversations about family traditions, favorite seasonal reads, and plans for the impending holiday break. After the recent darkness overshadowing Hamlet, the joy filling the shop warmed Shelby's heart.

A lull in new arrivals gave her a chance to slip behind the front counter. Snagging a snickerdoodle cookie from the platter, Shelby sank gratefully onto the stool next to Lucy.

"Quite the turnout, huh?" Lucy remarked, her cobalt blue eyes twinkling with delight as she scanned the animated room. "Everyone's so excited for the holidays this year. It's like we all need some extra cheer."

Shelby nodded, swallowing a bite of the cinnamon-dusted treat. "After what's happened, I think people are determined to really appreciate time with friends and loved ones." She dropped her voice to a conspiratorial whisper. "And to buy lots of gifts from local shops like mine."

Both women giggled at the candid admission. Shelby didn't mind profiting a bit from the surging holiday spirit. She could use the financial cushion entering a new year that was sure to hold fresh surprises and challenges.

Glancing up, Shelby noticed Detective Whitely weaving purposefully through the crowd toward them. Her pulse quickened. She still wasn't entirely accustomed to seeing the normally reserved detective looking casual in faded jeans and a brown leather jacket.

"Hey, Travis," Lucy greeted him cheerfully. "Here for some holiday cheer and gifts?"

"And discounts on any murder mysteries you don't already own?" Shelby added with a playful grin.

Travis's expressive eyes crinkled faintly in that subtle way of his.

"Actually, I came to talk shop for a minute, if you have time," he told Shelby. She nodded, gesturing for one of the employees to mind the counter while she and Travis stepped away for more privacy with Harper following after them.

When they found a quiet corner near the staircase, Shelby leaned against the wall, surprised to realize she was holding her breath. Strange how even a brief interaction with this man could throw her off balance.

"I heard from the police chief over in Sweet Cove," Travis began without preamble. "Chief Martin and I are friends. He called to suggest that it could be useful for us to collaborate more directly."

Shelby's eyebrows shot up. She couldn't imagine why a police chief she didn't even know and who worked in a town thirty minutes away would take interest in her informal, occasional cooperation with Travis.

Seeing her confusion, Travis explained, "It seems you made an impression on some consultants Chief Martin relies on. A pair of sisters, one named Courtney Roseland, and the other is Angie. They told the chief that you have sharp instincts, you're insightful, thoughtful, a good researcher, and you pick up on details that other people miss."

Shelby froze as realization hit. This was all because of the zing of electrical energy that passed between her and her friend Courtney at the coffee shop the other day. The sensation was clearly more than some static electricity, but why had Courtney taken such an interest in it? What exactly was that sensation that felt like a current running between them? What did it mean?

Shelby's eyes went wide. Do the Roseland sisters have abilities like she does?

Harper purred at her.

"Did Chief Martin say anything else about me?" Shelby asked carefully. "Or about these consultants?"

Travis shook his head. "He was just singling you out as someone insightful who could be helpful to investigations around here." He smiled slightly. "I happen to agree."

Shelby's cheeks warmed at the compliment, but her thoughts raced as she considered the new information. She needed to speak with Courtney again soon.

She tuned back in as Travis was saying, "...so I wanted to ask if you're open to collaborating more. I could use those observational skills of yours."

He seemed to hold his breath, watching her face intently.

Despite lingering questions, Shelby managed a shy smile. "I'm glad to help in any way I can."

Relief flickered across Travis's face, but as he tried to return his features to a neutral expression, his eyes still shone with a warm glow. "Great. I'll be in touch."

With a meaningful look Shelby couldn't decipher, the detective turned to retrace his steps through the crowded room. She watched as he left the shop, her heart beating faster than the brief conversation warranted. Shaking herself, she headed to rejoin Lucy.

"So, what did Detective Dreamy want?" her friend whispered, waggling her eyebrows.

Shelby rolled her eyes. "A police chief he knows suggested we collaborate more, actually. But why the chief thinks I can contribute much, I really don't know..." She trailed off with an uncertain shrug.

Lucy smiled and gave her friend's arm a reassuring squeeze. "You've got this. Just trust those super senses of yours."

Before Shelby could worry any more about it, the next wave of customers descended on the shop and she lost herself in answering questions about titles and restocking rapidly dwindling selections. By the time the crowd finally thinned near closing time, Shelby was pleasantly exhausted.

She lingered chatting with the few remaining stragglers, including Patrice who was tidying up the drink counter. The bell over the door jingled again around 8:30 pm, and two men walked into the shop.

"Mr. Peacock, it's so good to see you," she greeted him warmly.

The man smiled, his eyes bright and happy. "This is my son Justin."

"Nice to meet you, Justin." Shelby shook his hand.

"You, too. I've heard a lot about you."

"And where is that wonderful cat of yours?" Peacock looked around and then saw Harper trotting over to greet him and receive some pats.

"I hope we haven't missed all the festivities." Peacock's gaze took in the depleted baked goods tray. "Though I see we're rather late for the sweets."

"You're not late at all. We're open until 10 pm tonight. And not to worry, there are more platters of cookies coming out right now. Hold on and I'll get them." Shelby retrieved the cookies stored in the workroom off the sales floor.

With a smile, Mr. Peacock reached for a gingerbread cookie. As he enjoyed the treat, Shelby studied him closely. Some of the strain around his eyes had eased recently, though he remained wan and subdued compared to his usual lively self. The shadow cast by his close brush with death and from knowing he was still in danger continued to linger.

"It's nice your son could join you tonight," she said, recalling that Justin Peacock was also a lawyer.

"Justin rushed right up from Texas after that man was killed in my house. He was the one who suggested I get the security system installed."

"I thought it was the smart thing to do." Justin sipped from a mug of cocoa. "After hearing that my father's life might be in danger, I flew up here as soon as I could."

Mr. Peacock shook his head, dusting crumbs from his hands. "Justin insisted on coming up, but he can't neglect his law practice forever."

Justin smiled. "I'm doing fine working remotely. The firm can manage without me for a while."

Peacock smiled wistfully. "We've made some nice memories while he's been here. We've played chess, baked pies, and stayed up late reminiscing." His expression clouded. "Of course, I'd prefer if Justin still lived here, but I understand he has his own life."

"I'd love to come back here permanently. I'll be looking into it in the new year."

"That would be wonderful." Shelby smiled. She knew it would be great for Mr. Peacock to have his family close, but for now, at least Justin was only a phone call away.

Mr. Peacock brightened. "Enough chatter about us. Tell me how your holiday preparations are coming along, my dear."

As Shelby enthusiastically described how she and her parents would be decorating a towering Christmas tree soon and enjoying traditional baked treats with her grandparents, she felt Mr. Peacock's spirits lift. He reminded her so much of her own grandfather – kind, playful, and devoted to his family.

Their conversation was interrupted by another customer approaching.

Professor Rundle gave Mr. Peacock a hearty handshake and slap on the back. "Jim, you rascal! I heard chatter you'd been at the historical society gala and gave a reading. I'm so sorry I missed it. Too bad they didn't invite me to do a reading along with you. Oh, well, their loss."

Mr. Peacock's smile looked slightly forced. He shot Shelby an almost imperceptible eye roll over the professor's shoulder as the portly man laughed uproariously at his own wit.

Oblivious, Professor Rundle continued spraying spittle as he rambled loudly about the upcoming intercollegiate relay race he was sponsoring. Shelby noticed other patrons frowning in annoyance at his loud monologue.

When Rundle nearly exhausted his supply of self-important stories, Mr. Peacock managed to extract himself by pleading an early morning and the professor headed for the checkout counter.

"Quite a windbag, that one," Mr. Peacock

muttered once they were alone again. Seeing Shelby's surprise, he chuckled. "Oh yes, many people find Jeffrey's arrogance tiresome, but he's not a bad bloke ... just full of himself and looking to promote his accomplishments, loudly."

He gave Shelby's shoulder a paternal pat. "Thank you again for the treats, my dear, and for brightening my spirits with your charming company and lovely shop. Justin and I are going to browse for some gifts now."

Shelby impulsively hugged the older man, her heart full of fondness. As Mr. Peacock ambled off to look at the books and merchandise, she hoped he would find some peace and joy this holiday season despite the lingering shadows. He deserved it.

When Peacock and his son were ready to leave with their purchases, Shelby slipped them a few extra gingerbread cookies for the walk home.

When the shop closed, the next hour passed quickly as Shelby, Lucy, and two other staff members finished the closing tasks while Patrice counted the till.

Soon Shelby was climbing the stairs to her cozy apartment and warm bed, pleasantly exhausted. With Harper by her side, she fell asleep smiling, replaying images of children excitedly grabbing new books and people lingering to chat over mugs of cocoa.

Simple gifts that meant everything.

15

Shelby gazed out the passenger window as Lucy drove them along the scenic coastal road toward Sweet Cove. Despite the overcast winter sky, glimpses of the glittering ocean through the pines lifted her spirits. She was grateful Lucy had readily agreed to this short impromptu trip.

"Remember freshman year when we came to Sweet Cove for the huge end of summer beach bonfire?" Lucy asked, voicing Shelby's own nostalgic thoughts.

Shelby smiled, visions of a younger Courtney Roseland dancing barefoot by the firelight flashing through her mind. "We laughed so hard we nearly choked on our s'mores. She lived in Boston back then. It's nice the four sisters moved to Sweet Cove together."

She leaned back contentedly in her seat. "Courtney was one of the first friends I made at college. We hit it off right away – we were both bookworms and loved the ocean. I was shy around new people, but Courtney was always a ray of sunshine. She introduced me to her other friends and helped me fit in. We were both bursting with big plans and dreams."

Lucy nodded, her eyes warm with fond recollection. "You two were so cute, thick as thieves. The three of us had some great adventures together."

Shelby and Courtney were in some of the same clubs, the photography club, the business club, and the volleyball club. They had so much fun going to dances, meeting for coffee, and hanging out together with other friends. Courtney had a great sense of humor and was always helpful and kind.

They spent the remainder of the half-hour drive reminiscing about their college antics until the sparkling harbor and colorful storefronts of picturesque Sweet Cove came into view. Lucy easily found a parking spot near the charming brick sidewalks threading through downtown. The storefronts of the lovely downtown village were decorated with wreaths, ornaments, greens, and little white lights.

"I'll do some gift shopping so you and Courtney can catch up," Lucy said, waving Shelby toward the impressive Victorian mansion that was her destination. "Meet back in a couple of hours or so? Text me when you're done."

Shelby walked down Beach Street and hurried up the shoveled walkway, taking in the graceful turret and sprawling wraparound porch dotted with rocking chairs. Garlands of fragrant pine roping wound around the railings, and the decorations made the house resemble an elaborate gingerbread confection. Courtney's sister Ellie ran a bed and breakfast inn out of part of the huge house.

Before she could even knock, the front door was thrown open. Courtney hurried forward to envelop Shelby in an exuberant hug. Laughing, Shelby returned the embrace, once more feeling that intriguing zap of energy pass between them.

Courtney drew back, her eyes dancing. "I'm so excited you came to visit. Come in, I've got the sunroom all set up for us. Angie is working at her bakery, so she won't be joining us, but she sends greetings."

Shelby stepped inside the spacious foyer with its gleaming wood floors and crystal chandelier and stared at the enormous Christmas tree soaring into the air.

"That tree is gorgeous."

"Thanks. You wouldn't believe how long it took to decorate that thing." Courtney laughed. "Ellie always wants to do Christmas up big."

Following her friend to the sunroom at the side of the house, Shelby admired the elegant holiday decorations adorning every surface. She could easily imagine staying in the luxurious home as a pampered guest.

The sunny solarium was equally inviting with plush seating and a crackling fire chasing away the December chill. Soon the two friends were sitting comfortably on the sofas while sipping steaming mugs of cinnamon cocoa. Euclid, the family's giant orange Maine Coon, immediately leapt onto Courtney's lap, purring as the young woman stroked his glossy fur. Circe the black cat with a little white spot on her chest jumped up to sit with Shelby.

"I should have brought Harper to see you two," she told the cats.

"It's so good to catch up," Courtney said, smiling

fondly at Shelby. "I want to hear everything that's new." Her face became serious. "But first – you can ask me anything."

Shelby gathered her thoughts. She still felt somewhat intimidated bringing up the sensitive subject, wary of putting off her friend, but she couldn't ignore the mysteries surrounding Courtney and her sisters.

"You told the Sweet Cove chief of police I could help with investigations," Shelby began carefully, "because I have useful ... intuition?"

Courtney's expression turned serious, but her tone remained warm. "That's right. Angie agrees with me that you have keen observational abilities like we do."

She met Shelby's guarded gaze. "It's okay, Shelby. We're both dancing around the subject. You and I have some skills that most other people don't. I could feel it from you when we met in Hamlet. I know you have questions. Please just ask me."

Bolstered by her friend's openness, Shelby took a sip of cocoa before responding. "When we ran into each other, I felt this ... energy pass between us. And you clearly recognized something in me. Are you ... psychic?"

Courtney nodded solemnly. "I am. So are Angie and our other sisters. We all have extrasensory capabilities of varying kinds. Jenna can see ghosts and Ellie has telekinesis. That sure has come in handy at times." She smiled slightly. "So, when I felt your energy, I knew you were one of us."

Stunned, Shelby slowly absorbed this admission. Her suspicions were true - the Roseland sisters possessed the same unusual powers that were awakening in herself. She desperately hoped Courtney could provide answers about her own burgeoning abilities.

"How is this possible?" Shelby whispered. "I always thought people with psychic powers had them from birth."

Courtney shrugged, settling back against the cushions. "I don't claim to understand it fully. The women in our family are descended from a long line of intuits and healers ... women with remarkable gifts." She shook her head wonderingly. "But our talents laid dormant until we moved to Sweet Cove several years ago. Something about this town brought our latent senses to life."

Shelby shivered as pieces rapidly clicked together. "Hamlet has always been known to be a magical place," she mused. "I always accepted that some people in town had paranormal abilities, but I never thought I'd be one of them."

Courtney nodded excitedly. "I'm certain these seacoast towns nourish those of us with predispositions to the paranormal. Your skills will only grow stronger here."

Shelby finished the cocoa in her mug and set it aside. "Please, I want to understand. How do your abilities work? Have you always embraced them?"

Courtney nodded for Shelby to refill their mugs from the waiting carafe as she gathered her thoughts. The next hour flew by as Courtney described in fascinating detail her family's journey navigating their psychic gifts, the unique powers each sister possessed, and how they now assisted the Sweet Cove police department on cases. "Not many know about our skills. We keep it quiet for the most part. We only tell people we know we can trust. When we met you in Hamlet the other day, I could feel the electricity coming off of you. I knew something must have happened to you."

Shelby explained about her fall from the ladder and how when she came to, she could hear Harper talking to her mind. "No one else can hear Harper. Only me." She told Courtney how she could smell smoke before the Harris Estate mansion was set on fire. "I seem to notice things that others don't."

Shelby's heart swelled with hope. Courtney's experiences paralleled her own in uncanny ways. For the first time since her world shifted, Shelby didn't feel alone in the darkness.

"I'm still figuring all of this out," she admitted once Courtney had finished her incredible tale. "Any advice you have would mean the world."

Courtney nodded reassuringly. "It's a huge change, but you'll learn to manage your skills. Just don't push too hard. Let things unfold at their own pace. Hamlet is a special town filled with people who have abilities like ours. It's a good place for you to be." Her eyes took on a knowing gleam. "And that handsome detective you're assisting? He clearly cares about you. Let him support you on your journey."

Shelby's cheeks grew warm, but she tucked away Courtney's words about Travis to ponder later. For now, she had a million more questions about the amazing new reality she found herself in. The time with Courtney flew by in a blur.

All too soon, the friends parted with fierce hugs and promises to meet again soon. "Call me anytime if you need advice or you just want to talk,"

Courtney told her friend. "It's a huge change to deal with, but I love my skills and we love helping Chief Martin on cases. We all think it's important to use our powers for good."

Watching Courtney wave enthusiastically from the porch, Shelby carried away a glowing sense of belonging she hadn't felt in a long time.

She quickly located Lucy in town loaded down with shopping bags. Her head still spun from the wealth of information and advice Courtney had shared so openly.

"So? How did it go?" Lucy asked, glancing over with a knowing smile as she walked beside her friend. "You look ... lighter somehow."

"It was amazing." Shelby's voice was full of excitement as she took some of the bags from Lucy. "Courtney helped me understand so much. It seems I'm part of something extraordinary." Impulsively, she reached over to squeeze her friend's arm. "Thank you for convincing me to reach out to her. I feel like I can handle whatever comes next."

Lucy's answering smile shone bright. "All of this is so amazing, Shelby."

Spying a cozy restaurant, Shelby suggested, "Let's get dinner. I'm craving something comforting after such an emotional day."

Soon they were tucking into generous plates of pot roast, buttery mashed potatoes, and roasted vegetables. Between bites, Shelby eagerly recounted everything she had learned from Courtney, and saying the revelations out loud helped cement them as her new reality.

Across the checked tablecloth, Lucy's eyes shone. "You're embracing your powers. No more hiding or fear." She raised her glass of local hard cider. "Here's to you, mystic maven of Hamlet."

Laughing, Shelby clinked their glasses together.

When they were done with dinner, they stepped back outside into the velvety night, their breath clouding in the chill air. A sense of purpose settled deep into Shelby's bones. No more wavering. She had gifts to watch grow.

They drove in silence for a while with fields and woodlands rolling by, and soon the cozy shops and restaurants of downtown Hamlet came into view. Lucy easily maneuvered into a prime parking spot along the brick sidewalks near the bookshop.

Shelby stepped onto the pavement and turned in a slow circle, seeing her beloved town with fresh eyes. The quaint buildings, twinkling lights, and welcoming faces took on new meaning now that she understood more of the hidden side of this special town. Hamlet was more than home - it was the place where she would reach her potential.

Shelby strode briskly toward Spellbound Books, ready to write her next chapter. And she intended to shine.

16

Shelby breathed deeply, inhaling the familiar scents of paper, leather, and beeswax polish as she entered the stately public library. Stained glass windows cast patterns across the reading tables where patrons sat poring over books. Shelby nodded greetings to the white-haired woman manning the front desk before heading downstairs where the local historical archives were located.

The heels of her boots sank into the plush carpet as she navigated between the huge oak shelves holding the town's centuries-worth of records and found Justin Peacock seated alone at a table staring at the text filling his laptop screen. When Shelby approached, he glanced up, his features easing into a warm smile.

"Shelby, so nice to see you." He half-rose before sitting back into the leather chair. "Please, sit. I could use a break from estate law reports."

Shelby pulled out the adjacent seat, watching him roll his head and neck wearily. "Hard at work, I see. How's your remote arrangement going?"

Justin blew out a long sigh. "I can't complain. The firm back in Austin has been very accommodating. Though legal briefs don't make for exciting reading."

Shelby's gaze dropped to the hefty book open in front of him - a genealogy of Hamlet's founding families, she noted with interest. Justin followed her look and chuckled.

"Just a bit of light research on my ancestry to take a breather – just like my dad. We Peacocks didn't venture to the New World until the mid-1700s. We were latecomers compared to many families here."

His face brightened. "But speaking of family, Dad seems in good spirits. He's interested in planting more perennials in the spring so he's reading up on them, and I even convinced him to submit some new short fiction pieces."

Shelby beamed, glad to hear Mr. Peacock was regaining his usual cheer. "That's wonderful. Writing always recharges him. Please tell him I can't wait to read his new work."

Justin nodded, looking thoughtful. "Your friendship has meant the world to him, especially through this ordeal. You have a devoted admirer." His expression turned somber. "It comforts Dad to be back to familiar routines, but I still worry." He hesitated before continuing quietly. "What if the maniac who targeted him isn't finished? The lack of answers picks at me."

Shelby gave him a sympathetic nod. "The police are pursuing every lead. I have to believe they'll catch whoever is responsible before they can hurt your father or anyone else."

Justin searched her face, seeming to take heart from her determined tone. "You're likely right. I do get moments of despair. I just wish none of this had happened. Dad deserves to feel safe in the home he loves. I hate to leave him by himself but I have to get back to Texas."

"That's understandable. Your father does have many friends in town, if that's any consolation." Shelby asked gently, "Could you tell me more about your father's interests and the people in his circle in case anything proves relevant? And also if there's anyone you might consider as a suspect?"

Justin nodded; his brow furrowed in concentration. "Let's see ... as you probably know, he adores music. He plays clarinet with a local band. He's quite good actually. He's also passionate about numismatics - collecting and studying rare coins."

Shelby made careful mental notes as he continued.

"Gardening and of course, writing, as I mentioned. And games - chess, backgammon, cards. He'll play for hours given a willing partner."

Justin smiled faintly before growing serious once more. "As for professional connections, there were a few colleagues who resented Dad's courtroom success. One in particular, Felix Duncan, made some bitter remarks when they crossed paths after Dad's retirement."

Shelby leaned forward, intrigued. According to Justin, Felix took losing to Mr. Peacock badly and blamed the kindly man for stalling his career advancement. Though likely just an outburst by a poor sport, she added Duncan's name to the short list of potential suspects.

"You might want to speak to Dad's housekeeper, Polly Sutter. She comes in to clean once or twice a week. She even does some other tasks when Dad needs something."

"What sort of tasks?"

"Answering correspondence, picking up some things at the market, things like that."

"Anyone else you can think of who might hold a grudge against your father?"

"Some criminals Dad put away, maybe, but most of them are still incarcerated, as far as I know."

"How does your father get along with Professor Rundle?"

Justin smiled. "The professor is a bit of a windbag, always bragging about himself, but I think the man is jealous of my father. As far as wanting to kill him, I'd say that was very unlikely. I don't think the man would ever hurt anyone."

By the time Justin concluded summarizing his father's many interests and acquaintances, Shelby's head hummed with a couple of new avenues to explore. She hoped some seemingly minor detail might lead to the killer.

"This has been really helpful," she told Justin warmly as she packed her notebook and pen into her handbag. "Please tell your father I can hardly wait for his next literary event at the bookshop, and that his fans are eagerly awaiting his new work."

Justin walked her upstairs, appearing more relaxed despite the lingering worry haunting his eyes. He even joked with Shelby. "I'll let Dad know he has assignments waiting for him to do. He'll be delighted."

At the massive carved doors, he touched Shelby's shoulder. "Truly, thank you. Knowing that Dad has friends like you who want to help him gives me hope." Giving her hand a grateful squeeze, he strode off toward his car in the parking lot.

Shelby watched him go. They'd had a good conversation. Turning to leave the lot and head toward Spellbound Bookshop, Shelby's thoughts drifted to the housekeeper Justin had mentioned his father employing. She hadn't even realized Mr. Peacock had domestic help and was immediately curious what the woman might know of the household's comings and goings.

She dug the business card Justin had given her from her bag and dialed the housekeeper's number. After two rings, a female voice answered.

"Hello."

"Hi, Polly, I'm Shelby Price calling on behalf of James Peacock. Would you have a few minutes to chat someday?" After explaining what she wanted to talk about, they agreed to meet the next day.

Shelby hurried down the sidewalk eager to get home and review her notes from the conversation with Justin. Cold wind nipped at her cheeks as she stepped onto the sidewalk and turned briskly toward the bookshop, but she'd only gone a block when she heard hurried footsteps behind her.

"Shelby, hold up a sec!"

She turned in surprise to see Travis jogging to catch up, his cheeks flushed crimson from the chill. Tamping down the butterflies that awoke in her stomach, Shelby stopped to let him fall into step beside her.

"Travis, hi. What's up? Any news?"

He shook his head, flashing a rare boyish grin. "No, not yet. I was just headed to grab some coffee and thought I'd see if you'd join me." He hesitated briefly before adding, "To talk things over about collaborating on the case."

Shelby blinked, caught off guard by the casual invitation but she was secretly delighted. Time alone with Travis felt very appealing.

"I'd love that," she answered warmly. "How about Lucky's Café just down the block? Unless you had another place in mind."

"Lead the way." Travis gestured her forward with a smile.

Shelby tried but failed to ignore the pleasant flip-flop of her heart as they strolled together down the lamp-lit street. Dusk was settling over the town and the cafés and shops glowed invitingly against the coming darkness. Strings of white lights and festive garlands above the sidewalks added to the pretty scene.

Though the circumstances were less than joyful, Shelby couldn't deny the flicker of lightheartedness at being in Travis's company. She snuck a glance at his handsome profile and had to tamp down a grin. Get it together, she scolded herself. This was just two colleagues meeting to discuss a case, nothing more.

Lucky's cozy interior met them with warmth and the tempting scents of roasted coffee and sweet pastries. Keeping her expression neutral, Shelby let Travis select a small corner table before she headed to the counter to order for both of them.

Was meeting for coffee skirting the edges of something more than a professional chat? She wondered.

Holding two large steaming mugs, she pushed her thoughts to the back of her mind and joined Travis at the table tucked away from the door. He gave an appreciative sniff as she set the coffee before him.

"A cop's best friend," he proclaimed, wrapping

both hands around the toasty ceramic mug. Their knees brushed under the small bistro table sending Shelby's pesky pulse into overdrive again.

She took a bracing sip of her own lavender latte and tried to sound casual. "Sometimes, I like grabbing coffee here to clear my head after working all day in the bookshop." She gave him a look. "Do you bring all your consulting civilians out for coffee?"

Travis's eyebrows lifted in that subtly amused way she found so appealing. "Since I only have one civilian consultant, I guess the answer is yes."

Heat bloomed under Shelby's collar, and she knew a telltale blush colored her cheeks. Somehow Travis managed to disarm her without even trying. She stumbled to say something before flames could be seen in her eyes.

"Did you know Mr. Peacock employed a housekeeper? Her name's Polly Sutter. She does some odd tasks for him in addition to cleaning the house. I'm meeting her tomorrow."

Travis nodded. "I did speak to her, but she didn't offer anything helpful. You might be able to get more from her than I did." He took another sip of coffee, his gaze thoughtful. "I appreciate you setting up a meeting with her. Knowing who comes and goes from his home could prove useful."

Shelby nodded, encouraged that her initiative to interview Polly had been on the right track. When a staff member at the café carried a tray of fresh muffins to the glass case, Shelby suggested they get some and rose briefly to get two plump cranberry muffins from the counter, thinking Travis could use something to eat. She herself often forgot meals when she was preoccupied with a project.

His appreciative smile when she set the baked goods between them caused a swarm of butterflies to take flight in her midsection again.

She said breezily, "Can't go wrong with Lucky's famous cranberry muffins. They're addictive."

She let the conversation lapse into a comfortable silence for a few minutes, enjoying the muffin and Travis's companionship. Nearby patrons chatted and chuckled over their own treats and drinks, creating a cheerful ambiance.

When she finished her muffin, Shelby dusted the crumbs from her hands and turned a thoughtful gaze to Travis. "Do you think it's possible the murderer could be someone angry or jealous of Mr. Peacock's successful career or an old courtroom rival, maybe?"

Travis took a sip before responding. "We're certainly looking into any past legal connections that went sour. Jealousy over reputation or lost cases can fester." He rotated the nearly empty mug between his large hands.

Shelby bit her lip, mulling this over. "What if it's someone closer to home - say that blustery Professor Rundle? He seems to crave the limelight. Could it be that he secretly resents Mr. Peacock's success and reputation in this town?"

One dark eyebrow quirked upward. "Interesting theory. I admit the man's overbearing personality rubs me the wrong way, too." Travis sat back with a sigh. "But right now, we have no solid evidence implicating the professor or anyone else. It's all just conjecture for the moment."

Shelby nodded reluctantly, understanding it would take more than speculation to pin down a suspect. She stirred a dash more milk into her drink, grasping for any scrap that could help the case. Glancing up, she noticed Travis watching her with a strange expression she couldn't quite decipher. Was that ... admiration maybe?

"We'll get there," he said suddenly, firm confidence resonating in his deep voice. "You have good instincts, Shelby. Together, we'll find the clues we need."

Unexpected emotion squeezed her throat at his

faith in her uncertain talents, and his choice of the word "together." Before she did something mortifying, Shelby gathered their empty mugs.

"Refills? It's on me," she managed, blinking hard.

"That would be great." Travis's little smile made her pulse skitter all over again. He held her gaze an extra beat. "And Shelby? Don't underestimate yourself. You're one of the sharpest investigators I've had the privilege to work with."

Now she knew a fiery blush colored her whole face so she simply turned and scurried to the counter on jelly legs. Had he really just called her a talented investigator? His unexpected praise threatened to dissolve her strictly professional resolve, especially with the handsome face smiling up at her so warmly.

Shelby sucked in a deep breath and got in line, gripping the empty mugs tightly. So what if they shared an easy rapport and unspoken connection? And sure, the setting felt cozily date-like, but she couldn't lose focus and make things out to be more than they were. They had a job to do. She couldn't afford a crush on the lead detective who relied on her for impartial insights.

By the time she returned to the table having pep-talked herself out of mooning over Travis, Shelby felt composed and business-like. She set down the fresh coffees and took out her notebook flipping to a blank page. Time to demonstrate her serious investigative skills.

"Okay, maybe we're going about this all wrong with the list of suspects," she mused aloud. Travis raised his eyebrows but gestured for her to continue.

"What if there's some physical location that holds the key?" Shelby tapped her pen as her thoughts raced. "Something connected to Mr. Peacock we haven't explored yet."

Understanding flashed across Travis's face and he sat forward. "You're right. We've been so focused on the Harris Estate and Peacock's law career; we haven't dug much into other aspects."

His boyish grin made a brief appearance. "This is why it's good to have you around. You see things from a different perspective. We need to get out of our heads and re-examine the spaces tied to Mr. Peacock with fresh eyes."

Shelby flushed with pleasure at having sparked a new investigative angle. "Should we sit down with Mr. Peacock and map out everywhere he frequents? Maybe something will trigger a new lead."

"Sounds like a plan." Travis beamed at the young woman. "You're really something else, Shelby Price."

His words sent lightning zipping through Shelby's body. She froze, afraid to even breathe for fear of shattering the fragile moment. Travis seemed equally immobilized, and the air between them fairly crackled with awareness and possibilities.

Abruptly Travis pulled back, looking uncharacteristically flustered. He fumbled for his wallet, nearly upending what remained of his coffee. "We, uh, we should call it a night. Early shift tomorrow and all that."

Shelby sat motionless, her pulse hammering in her ears. Travis avoided her eyes as he stood, tossing cash on the table.

"Can you update me after you've spoken to Mr. Peacock? About important locations?" His professional demeanor had snapped back into place with only the tips of his ears still tinged faintly pink.

Shelby nodded.

Travis gave her a brief, formal smile that didn't reach his eyes. "Great. Well, good work today. I'll be in touch."

And with that, he was striding out the door. Shelby, pondering her confused emotions, collected herself and left the café.

The bracing winter air hit her like a splash of icy water jolting her the rest of the way back to a clear head. She stood uncertainly on the sidewalk for a moment. Had she only imagined a moment of connection with Travis?

With a sigh, Shelby turned toward home and the bookshop. There was an investigation to pursue and a kind man's life was still in jeopardy. Anything more personal would have to wait.

As she walked, Shelby touched tentative fingertips to her traitorous left hand, still tingling faintly from Travis's brief grasp. Her logical mind scolded against indulging in girlish notions, but her heart whispered that maybe when the case was over....

For now, she simply drew her coat tighter against the cold and picked up her pace. The rest would have to bide its time.

Reaching the shop, Shelby unlocked the front door and headed straight for her office.

Leaning back in her office chair, she tapped her pen against the notes spread before her. Frustration simmered in her veins as nothing jumped out at her. She made a few more notes about the meeting with Justin on a fresh page of her notebook, recording what she'd learned. She believed each small puzzle piece would eventually draw her closer to completing the picture.

Glancing at the wall clock, she decided to go up

to her apartment and spend the evening brainstorming. Shelby headed upstairs to settle onto the sofa with Harper, a well-worn blanket, and a notepad as thoughts spun around in her head.

She told the cat about her meeting with Travis. "I think I misinterpreted what was going on between us."

Harper blinked sleepily. "Be patient, Shelby. Some things can't be rushed."

17

Warm light spilled from the windows of Shelby's parents' cozy farmhouse onto the snowy yard, welcoming her back to her childhood home. She stomped the slush off her boots before entering the warmth of the house where she'd grown up, just a fifteen-minute drive from the center of Hamlet.

Shelby breathed deep, inhaling the mingled scents of fir and cinnamon as she stepped into the kitchen with Harper trotting after her.

"Yoo-hoo, we're back here," her mother called from the direction of the living room.

Grinning, Shelby made her way past the cheery red and green decorations adorning practically every surface and found her family gathered around a massive fir tree that nearly brushed the high ceiling.

"Shelby!" Her father enveloped her in a long hug. The man always greeted his daughter as if she'd just returned from years away. At seventy-two-years-old, John Price remained hale and hardy thanks to a life of physical labor working on their family farm. The man was a retired teacher, but he'd run the farm since he was in his twenties growing sunflowers, vegetables, and pumpkins. His lined face crinkled into a smile beneath the brim of his ever-present cap.

"Let me see this beautiful cat." He bent to scratch Harper behind the ears as she rubbed against his leg, purring. "What a fine cat you are, Harper," he told the feline as his eyes twinkled merrily.

Shelby just laughed as her no-nonsense father petted the soft animal. Like all of the Price clan, once he decided you were family, he loved you unconditionally.

Her mother bustled over a few strands of silver-streaked brown hair escaping from her messy bun. "How are you, hon?" Ginny asked, standing up on tiptoes to kiss Shelby's cheek. "I'm glad to hear your holiday sale party went so well."

At sixty-nine, her mom, also a retired teacher, remained the hub of the family. She delighted in gathering her brood for cherished rituals like trimming the tree while drinking wassail punch and making popcorn garlands. Shelby smiled, taking a deep breath of the wonderful pine scent.

Soon she was cheerfully accepting a mug of hot cider and joining in the festive chaos. Her older brother Adam untangled strings of twinkling lights while his girlfriend Lauren helped to unwrap the cherished ornaments that had been handed down for generations.

On the sofa, Shelby's maternal grandparents, Mary and Tom, who also lived in the farmhouse, sipped from their own steaming mugs. At ninety-three, Tom's hearing wasn't what it used to be, but his leathery face still displayed a mischievous grin as he watched his family's antics. Beside him, Mary smiled and greeted Shelby while patting her husband's knee with her hand.

Shelby's heart swelled just soaking up the familial energy swirling through the cheery living room.

Lauren put on some Christmas carols and soon boisterous off-key singing filled the room. Shelby held the ladder steady as her father clambered up to position the antique angel at the tree top. The way his weathered hands gently straightened the delicate wings, made Shelby smile brightly. They all helped place the white lights, small red bows, and ornaments on the branches, and later with the decorating complete, Ginny shooed them all toward the groaning farm table laden with juicy pot roast, buttery mashed potatoes, sweet glazed carrots, and yeasty rolls. Over steaming cups of wassail, the conversation soon turned to updates on various family members Shelby hadn't seen for a couple of weeks.

She was describing the next holiday bookshop event to everyone when Ginny's expression sharpened with interest. "Oh, that reminds me, I had coffee with Patrice Nelson from your store the other day. We got to discussing poor Mr. Peacock."

Shelby leaned in, intrigued. "Did Patrice mention anything that could help with the investigation? The police keep hitting dead ends trying to find out who's targeting Mr. Peacock."

Ginny pursed her lips, thinking. "Not really. She said James has been writing and working part-time at the library. He's researching an unsolved cold case about a murder that happened in town about twenty years ago. He's trying to keep busy so his thoughts don't stray too often to the lunatic who is targeting him. You must have heard he had a security system installed. That must give him some peace of mind."

Shelby sat back, digesting the information thoughtfully. She recalled Justin mentioning his father's work writing several articles and a new book. He also mentioned Mr. Peacock's renewed interest in gardening and that he was designing some yard space for more perennials. "I talked to Mr. Peacock's son the other day. He told me his dad loves playing cards and chess, collecting rare coins, and playing clarinet in a band. He has a lot of interests."

"His wide interests bring him in contact with a lot of different people which makes it hard to pin down a suspect," Ginny pointed out. The woman loved reading mystery novels and had a knack for figuring out the storylines. "The killer must be someone James knows."

The whole family knew that Shelby was working as a volunteer consultant with the police, but none of them knew about her newly awakening paranormal skills. She planned to tell them, but it never seemed like the right time. Plus, she didn't want them to think she was losing her mind.

Shelby said, "Thanks, Mom, that's really helpful. I'll talk to Detective Whitely about it."

Ginny hugged her daughter. "Ever since you were little, you've had such a strong sense of justice, and right and wrong. I'm glad you're finding ways to act on it. You're doing important work, Shelby Lee. I couldn't be prouder."

Blinking back some sentimental tears, Shelby gratefully squeezed her mom's hand. She was determined not to let them down.

After dinner, the party moved to the cozy den for boisterous games of charades, cards, carol singing accompanied by her dad on guitar, and watching nostalgic holiday specials. As the clock struck midnight, Shelby's grandparents headed off to their bedroom after goodbyes were exchanged with hearty hugs.

Shelby headed out into the star-strewn darkness with Harper curled in her arms and a bag filled with containers of leftovers. The drive home along moonlit deserted country lanes never failed to make Shelby happy.

Back in her snug apartment, she got ready for bed feeling more centered than she had in weeks. The time with her family never failed to steady her when inner turmoil or outside forces unsettled her.

Slipping under the covers with Harper snoozing right beside her, Shelby switched off the bedside lamp and lay gazing up through the skylight. A rare cloudless night revealed what looked like millions of glittering pinpricks in the black canopy above her. Shelby imagined family members who had passed away spinning far out in the cosmos, their voices added to the celestial chorus lulling her to sleep.

But slumber remained elusive as her thoughts circled back to the man who occupied so much space in her mind these days - Travis. A vision of his face as they talked casually over coffee warmed her heart and she sighed.

Could exploring a deeper bond between them be worth the risk? Past experience made her hesitant to open her heart again, yet denying what she felt grew harder by the day.

The next morning, sleepiness still fogged Shelby's brain as she shuffled to the kitchen in fuzzy slippers to start the coffee. She was sitting at the kitchen table reading news on her phone when a knock sounded on the door. Shelby went to answer it and saw her mother standing on the porch.

"Hey, Mom. You're up early."

Ginny came in and set a bakery box on the counter. "Your dad has been craving some chocolate croissants from Bread and Roses Bakery, so I came to town to get some for him. I thought you might like some, too." She bent to pat the cat. "Good morning, Harper." Ginny got two plates from the cabinet and placed a croissant on each one as Shelby poured two cups of coffee.

The woman's sharp gaze assessed Shelby over the rim of the cup she sipped from. "You look preoccupied this morning."

Shelby took a gulp of coffee, bracing to tell her mother about the problem occupying her thoughts. "I couldn't turn my brain off last night. I kept mulling over a, well, personal issue." She hesitated before blurting out, "It's about Travis - Detective Whitely."

Ginny regarded her, waiting for her daughter to continue.

Plunging ahead, Shelby described her deepening feelings for Travis and their recent intense chemistry. "But after some bad relationships, especially the last one, I'm wary of being hurt again," she concluded softly.

Setting down her coffee cup, Ginny reached over to squeeze Shelby's hand. "You've always been open-hearted - it's one of your finest qualities, but it can also be your Achilles' heel."

Shelby looked up and saw understanding in her mom's wise eyes.

"I know you're cautious giving your affections after what happened in your last relationship. It's never easy to be cheated on. It can take a long while to get past that." Ginny shook her head, scowling briefly at the memory of the man who had callously broken Shelby's heart and trust two years prior.

"But don't sacrifice future happiness because of one cad's misdeeds," she continued gently. "Good men do exist, though they seem rarer than hen's teeth sometimes." She smiled encouragingly. "From all you've told me, Travis strikes me as one of the good ones. If you feel a connection, love is always a chance worth taking."

Shelby's eyes misted over and a lump formed in her throat. Impulsively she circled the table to hug her mother. "I'm still scared of getting hurt again," she whispered shakily, "but being close to Travis makes me feel brave, and he seems to really believe in me."

"Then it seems you have your answer." Ginny rubbed her back consolingly. "Take your time and see where it leads. I just want to see you living a rich and happy life."

Shelby drew back, smiling. "I'll think it over. My heart and head haven't quite agreed yet. Thanks for wanting me to be happy, Mom."

Ginny waved off her thanks. "You'll do what's right for you when the time comes. For now, let's eat these chocolate croissants while I pour us more coffee."

The rest of their time passed enjoyably discussing other topics, but later on in the bookshop, Shelby replayed her mother's words on repeat.

Love is a chance worth taking.

She couldn't deny the risks of opening herself to someone, but maybe the good of being with someone like Travis might be worth a leap of faith.

She looked out the window at the bracing winter sky. The clouds going by seemed like her scattered thoughts - constantly shifting and reforming.

"Your mother's right, you know," Harper said from her sunlit perch on the windowsill. "You can't let one bad apple keep you from finding happiness. Be patient. All will unfold as it should."

Shelby reached out and moved her hand over the cat's soft fur. She would hold her mother's and Harper's words in her heart.

18

Shelby pulled up to the small ranch house on Elm Street just outside the village of Hamlet in Forestdale and checked the address against the one Justin Peacock had given her for his father's housekeeper, Polly Sutter. Seeing it matched, she walked up to the front door and rang the bell.

A minute later, the door opened to reveal a petite woman with long auburn hair pulled back in a ponytail. She looked to be in her mid-thirties and was dressed casually in jeans and a sweater.

"Hi, are you Polly Sutter?" Shelby inquired.

"You must be Shelby," the woman said.

Shelby nodded. "I'm Shelby Price. I'm a friend of James Peacock. I was hoping to ask you a few questions about him and the work you do for him."

Polly's expression turned wary. "Has something happened? Is Mr. Peacock all right?"

Shelby reassured her, "Oh, he's fine. I just have some questions about his routine and was hoping you could help me get a better picture of his life. I'm assisting the Hamlet Police with some interviews."

Polly considered this for a moment before stepping back and opening the door wider. "All right, come on in. Can I get you something to drink? I just brewed some tea."

"Tea would be great, thanks," Shelby said, stepping inside and following Polly to the small but tidy kitchen.

As Polly busied herself preparing two mugs of tea, Shelby took the opportunity to observe the housekeeper. She was petite, no more than five foot three, and quite fit with a trim figure. Her movements were efficient as she went about making the tea. Her fair skin was free of makeup except for a little mascara.

Soon they were seated across from each other at the kitchen table, steaming mugs before them.

Shelby took a sip of the fragrant Earl Grey before speaking. "I really appreciate you taking the time to talk with me, Ms. Sutter."

"Please, call me Polly," the housekeeper responded.

"How long have you worked for Mr. Peacock?"

"Let's see, I started with him about ... two years ago now," Polly said after a moment's thought. "Someone I knew used to clean for him, but then she moved away, so she recommended me to take over."

Shelby nodded. "What are your main responsibilities for Mr. Peacock?"

"Well, I go to his house once or twice a week to do a thorough cleaning - vacuuming, dusting, bathrooms, changing the sheets, that kind of thing," Polly explained. "I also stop by a few times a week just to pick up the mail and check on things, and if he needs some shopping done, like picking up groceries or dry cleaning or whatever, I do that too. Sometimes, I help him answer correspondence. Occasionally, I make dinner for him."

"So, you're like his personal assistant in a way?" Shelby suggested.

Polly looked pleased by this description. "I suppose so, yes. I like taking care of all those little details for him, so he doesn't have to worry about it. He's alone. His wife died a few years ago and his son lives in Texas."

"Does Mr. Peacock have many regular visitors to the house?" Shelby inquired.

The housekeeper thought for a moment. "Not a lot, but there are a few friends who come over fairly regularly. Let's see, there's Professor Rundle - he'll come by to have dinner once or twice a month, and there's William McManus and Vincent Manning who like to come over to play cards. Oh, and a woman named Julie Hall will visit and have tea with Mr. Peacock every couple of weeks."

Shelby nodded, noting the names. She knew Julie Hall worked at the town library.

"With everything that's happened, I have to admit I get a little nervous being alone in Mr. Peacock's house sometimes," Polly confessed. "I make sure to turn on the security system whenever I'm there now."

"That's understandable," Shelby said sympathetically. "Have you noticed any unusual people hanging around the neighborhood or anything suspicious going on?"

Polly shook her head. "No, nothing that I can recall, but I'm usually only there for about two hours at a time."

"Did you happen to stop by the house at all while

Mr. Peacock was away at his conference?" Shelby asked.

"Let's see ... yes, I went twice just to pick up his mail and do a quick tidy," Polly recalled. "I didn't notice anything amiss though."

Shelby decided to change tacks. "So, it sounds like you know Mr. Peacock and his routine pretty well after two years. What would you say his main interests and hobbies are?"

The housekeeper thought for a moment. "Well, he's quite the reader - always has a book going, and I know he enjoys writing in his spare time. He's published several books and lots of articles. He's also fond of playing cards and board games. Oh, and gardening - he's very proud of his vegetable garden and flower beds."

Polly smiled and continued, "He's also a collector. He's accumulated some lovely small seascapes painted by local artists, and he has a sizable collection of old coins that he's quite knowledgeable about."

"I see," said Shelby. "Have you ever seen his coin collection?"

"Just in passing. Sometimes, he sits at his desk with the collection books."

"What about the paintings he collects?" Shelby asked. "Does he have all of the paintings on display?"

Polly's forehead scrunched up in thought. "I'm not sure about that."

"And what about you, Polly? Are you married? Do you have family nearby?"

At this, the housekeeper's friendly demeanor cooled a bit. "No, I'm divorced, but that's really none of your concern." Her tone turned sharp. "The police already questioned me. I'm not a suspect here."

Shelby held up a hand in a conciliatory gesture. "You're absolutely right, I apologize. I didn't mean to pry into your personal life."

Polly's expression softened slightly. "It's fine. I don't mind answering questions about Mr. Peacock and my work for him, but my private life is off-limits, okay?"

"Of course," Shelby agreed. She decided not to push the issue further. Still, she wondered about the housekeeper's sudden defensiveness when asked about her own life. Shelby made a mental note to tread carefully around topics that Polly seemed sensitive about.

She finished her tea and stood up. "Well, thank you again for your time. You've been very helpful."

Polly walked her to the door. "I hope I was able to

give you some useful information about Mr. Peacock. I hope the police hurry up and find the killer who's after him. Please let me know if there's anything else I can do to help. I care about him very much."

"I will. Take care," Shelby said as she stepped outside.

As she drove away, Shelby mulled over what she had learned. Polly certainly seemed to have an affection for her employer as well as a desire to protect him, but could she be hiding something about her personal life that was relevant to the case?

Shelby wasn't sure but made a mental note to look more into Polly's background when she had the chance. For now, at least she had gained more insight into James Peacock's routines and relationships.

When she arrived home, Shelby pulled out her notebook and began jotting down the key details from her conversation with Polly. As she wrote, she talked to Harper about the visit to the woman reporting that the housekeeper had provided several useful pieces of information, including potential suspects like Professor Rundle who visited Peacock regularly. "Mr. Peacock has some friends he sees fairly often, and a woman from the library comes to the house for tea on occasion."

Harper turned to look at her human friend. "A woman? Well, well, maybe Mr. Peacock isn't as lonely as we thought he was."

"I never thought he was lonely," Shelby corrected the cat.

"I wish I'd been able to go with you to see Polly," Harper said to Shelby's mind. "I'd like to see what I thought of her. Do you think she was lying about any of it?"

"I didn't get that impression although it was weird that she refused to answer simple questions about herself."

"Did you try to use your skills to pick up on anything about her?"

Shelby sat quietly for a moment feeling sheepish that she didn't try to sense anything about Polly.

"Never mind," Harper told her. "In the future, when you're talking to people, try to turn on your extrasensory skills."

Shaking her head, Shelby said with a sigh, "Some paranormal psychic I am. I was so busy asking questions and listening to her answers that I didn't even think to use my paranormal abilities."

"Don't beat yourself up about it. All of this is new

to you. That's why I wish I had been there," Harper muttered.

Shelby needed to follow up on the leads. Despite forgetting to tap into her powers, she felt she was making progress in getting to know about the people closest to James Peacock and hopefully, in identifying who might wish him harm.

"I'd better talk to Travis about my meeting with Polly." As soon as Shelby had said his name, she felt little sparks dancing over her skin.

Stay professional, she told herself. *Stay professional.*

19

After pushing open the library's heavy wooden door, Shelby stomped snow off her boots and unwound her long woolen scarf. Spotting Julie Hall at the reference desk, she waved and made her way over.

At seventy-three-years old, Julie was an attractive woman, slender with chin-length silvery gray hair. She'd been the full-time librarian in Hamlet for decades before reducing her hours to part-time only a year ago. Two years prior, she'd lost her beloved husband of nearly fifty years.

"Hey, Julie, thanks for making the time to chat with me," Shelby said, giving the older woman a quick hug.

"Of course, dear. I'm happy to help if I can." Julie led them up the sweeping staircase to the second-floor meeting rooms. Settling at a table in the empty space, she fixed Shelby with a searching look.

"I know you're here to talk about James. That dreadful business at his home has me sick with worry. Have the police made any headway?"

Shelby quickly filled her in on the scant details known so far. "They still have no firm suspects, unfortunately."

Julie shook her head with her brows drawn together in concern. "This is troubling. And they have no idea yet who would wish James harm?"

"A few vague theories, but the police lack evidence," Shelby admitted with a sigh. "It's probably someone who knows him, so maybe a friend or acquaintance. That's why I hoped to get your take."

Julie nodded slowly, staring off at the snowy skyline visible through the tall windows. "James and I have become quite dear friends this past year," she said after a weighty pause. "After losing Harold, having James to talk with has meant the world to me. I have plenty of women friends, but I miss Harold terribly, and it's nice to have James to talk to about my loss since his wife passed away not that long ago. We're both in similar emotional states."

Shelby nodded. "He's lucky to have you to talk with."

"We have good conversations," Julie told the young woman. "We help one another with our grief and we enjoy each other's company. It helps to talk with someone who has also lost a partner. We meet for dinner or tea, take walks, visit museums, attend lectures together. I've been very worried about him after learning of the murder of that petty thief in his house. The killer must have been looking for James. The thought of him returning to hurt James makes a shiver run over my skin." She rubbed her arms trying to ward off the chill of concern. "How can I help? What can I tell you?"

Leaning forward, Shelby met Julie's eyes. "Have you noticed any friends who seem overly curious about James's life and assets lately? Even casual remarks could be telling."

Julie pursed her lips thinking back carefully before shaking her head. "I can't recall anything amiss. Most of his friends are harmless local gents who enjoy literature and history like James does." She smiled wistfully. "We even have a bit of book club going amongst all of us."

Shelby had to smile. Only in a quaint town like Hamlet would the murder suspect list contain book club members. She tapped her fingers on the table thinking aloud, "Still, we have to be missing something here. My gut says whoever is behind this is much closer than we realize. Detective Whitely has officers keeping an eye on Mr. Peacock's house," Shelby hastily assured the woman. "And I've been checking on him regularly too."

Julie nodded, taking this in. "I invited James to stay at my house in the spare bedroom, but he declined. He's too worried that he'd put me in danger, but that's James—always thinking of others before himself."

Shelby studied the older woman, struck by her graceful poise and intelligent eyes. "How are you holding up through all of this?"

Julie looked down, blinking rapidly before meeting Shelby's gaze. "Oh, I'm all right, I suppose. It's James I fret over day and night." Her eyes took on a faraway look. "Such a lovely man. We've become such good friends. My talks with James always lift my spirits."

A wistful smile crossed the woman's face. "He's been a blessing to me. We just click - chatting about books, current events, art, our families. Sometimes we sit in comfortable silence lost in our own thoughts." She shook her head. "I can't bear thinking of him coming to harm when he still has so much life left to live."

"The police are doing everything possible to ensure Mr. Peacock stays safe. We just have to keep faith."

Julie patted the young woman's hand gratefully. "You're a gem, Shelby. I can see why James adores you so – you have a very caring heart." She tilted her head thoughtfully. "Rather like Emily Harris come again after all these decades."

Shelby started slightly. "Emily Harris?"

"She owned your bookshop property over a century ago. Such a vibrant spirit, cut down far too soon by a thief in the night." Anger flashed in Julie's eyes.

Shelby looked at the woman with interest. "What more do you know about Emily Harris? Mr. Peacock has told me some things about her. I'd love to hear more of the history."

Julie settled back in her chair. "Emily was the only child of a rather well-off couple. She was strong-willed too - she scandalously turned down several suitors much to her parents' chagrin. Then when her parents died, she used her inheritance to open her own store. She was quite an independent woman."

"She owned the building that became Spellbound Books," Shelby said slowly.

Julie nodded. "Emily was quite the progressive businesswoman for the times. From what I've read, she was charming and vivacious by all accounts. She had many friends even if she steadfastly maintained her independence." Julie smiled wryly. "I rather see myself in her and have always felt an affinity."

Julie's expression darkened. "Unfortunately, her light was extinguished far too soon. Back then, everyone believed a vagrant robbed and murdered her, but not long ago, a historian uncovered evidence that it was someone Emily knew who committed the foul deed." She shook her head sadly. "It was her own lawyer who apparently killed her. He tried to pressure her into marriage so he could get his hands on her assets. Emily had quite a valuable stamp collection that he wanted. When she uncovered his scheme, he attacked and killed her. A true fiend."

As Shelby absorbed the new information, her thoughts were churning. "How awful. Her friend and defender turned betrayer." She met Julie's eyes.

The woman nodded grimly and sighed deeply before continuing in a lighter tone. "But let's speak of more cheerful things. Are you spending the holiday with your family this year, dear?"

Shelby smiled, following the change of subject. They passed another half hour in pleasant conversation about traditions, favorite carols, and cookie recipes.

When they finished their chat, Shelby went downstairs and wound slowly through the stacks. Rounding a corner into the empty and dimly lit classics wing, she trailed her fingers idly across the leather spines enjoying the nostalgic scent of old paper and binding glue.

Pausing to look at the titles on one of the shelves, she heard the sound of a male voice speaking in tight, bitter tones. Edging closer, she peered cautiously through a gap between the shelves at a tall, powerfully built man of about fifty pacing while gripping a cell phone to his ear. Even in profile, the set of his jaw showed anger and dissatisfaction.

Something about his threatening energy rooted her in place and she strained to make out the words as he carried on his tirade.

"That useless detective has nothing on me, but the D.A.'s office here protects their own." He practically spit out the words. "It doesn't matter if the mighty James Peacock is retired now. His cronies still stymie my career at every turn."

The man gave a contemptuous laugh. "I half hoped that intruder had finished Peacock off in his own home. Maybe the killer will come back and finish the job. I should have killed the old buzzard myself years ago. Slipped something into his drink maybe..."

Shelby's hand flew to her mouth at the chilling words. This had to be Felix Duncan, the bitter defense lawyer Justin Peacock mentioned when she'd met with him.

The man abruptly glanced over. Holding her breath, Shelby shrank back behind the shelf with her pulse racing. She held still, praying he hadn't spotted her.

After an agonizing minute, she finally heard furious footsteps moving toward the front door of the library. Slowly peering around the corner, she saw the aisle was empty.

Shelby sagged against a shelf, her legs feeling weak. She had to tell Travis what she'd heard.

Squaring her shoulders, she took a breath and strode outside into the swirling snow. She needed to talk to Travis ... and fast.

20

Shelby and Travis gazed appreciatively at the small seascapes lining the walls of James Peacock's living and dining rooms. The intricate oil paintings depicted ocean vistas and quaint coastal villages.

"These are lovely," she remarked. "You have quite an impressive collection."

Pleased, Mr. Peacock smiled. "Thank you. I've been collecting these for years, mainly from local artists. I love the ocean." He gestured to a painting of a ship. "That one's my favorite - the artist perfectly captured the feeling of being a small boat on an endless ocean."

Shelby studied it, noting the vivid brushwork. She could almost hear the cry of gulls and the crash of the waves.

"Now, let me show you my other pride and joy," Peacock said, leading them down the hall to a small study. He unlocked a glass-fronted cabinet to reveal neat rows of antique coins set in a velvet-lined box gleaming under the lights.

"Wow," breathed Shelby, leaning in for a closer look. The coins ranged from simple silver pieces to intricately engraved gold medallions, and some of them looked centuries old.

"This is just a small part of my collection," explained Peacock. "I've been fascinated with old coins since I was a boy. There's something about holding a piece of history in your hand. The stories they could tell."

Shelby nodded. She could understand the appeal of tangibly connecting to the past like that. As her eyes roamed over the coins, she was drawn to one in particular - a tarnished gold piece with a lion emblem.

"May I hold that one?"

Peacock brought over a pair of thin gloves for Shelby to put on. "It's important to wear the gloves to protect the coin."

Reaching out a hand, the young woman gently lifted it from the velvet slot and the instant her fingers touched the cool metal, Shelby sucked in a sharp breath. The room swam before her eyes and suddenly a vivid scene flashed in her mind - she saw a shadowy figure creeping through moonlit rooms going through drawers and cabinets. The person paused by the coin collection, greedily running their hands over the treasures. Shelby strained to see their face, but it remained obscured in the darkness.

Just as abruptly, the vision ended and Shelby sagged against Travis who stood beside her.

"Whoa, are you all right?" Travis grasped her shoulders to steady her as Mr. Peacock looked on in concern.

"Shelby, what happened?" asked Mr. Peacock worriedly.

Struggling to clear the fog from her brain, she was still disoriented from the intense vision. "I'm sorry ... I just felt lightheaded for a moment," she managed.

Travis helped ease her into a chair. "Put your head down between your knees," he advised. "Take slow, deep breaths."

As Shelby followed his instructions, her head gradually cleared. She couldn't very well tell them what had really happened - they'd think she was crazy if she reported that touching the coin had triggered a psychic vision.

"I'm so sorry to worry you," she said, slowly sitting back up. "I guess I didn't eat enough at breakfast, and I didn't sleep well last night." She shot Travis an apologetic look.

"No need to apologize," Mr. Peacock assured her kindly. "Let me get you some juice." The man bustled off to the kitchen.

Travis crouched beside her chair; his brown eyes filled with concern. "Are you sure you're okay? Can I get you anything?"

Shelby managed a wan smile. "I'll be fine. Thanks, Travis. I just need to get my blood sugar up."

They chatted casually about the coin collection to fill the time until Mr. Peacock returned with a glass of orange juice and a granola bar. After drinking the juice and eating the bar, Shelby felt much better.

"We should probably head out," Travis suggested. "It would probably be good for you to rest."

They bid Mr. Peacock goodbye with promises to meet again soon.

As they walked back into town, fat snowflakes

drifted lazily down from the steel gray sky. Shelby tucked her hands into her coat pockets and ducked her chin into her scarf to ward off the chill. She glanced around at the charming shopfronts lining Main Street each one decked out in holiday splendor. Gleaming garlands with red bows framed windows filled with festive displays. Sparkling white lights edged the eaves of the quaint buildings and Christmas trees seen through front windows were decorated with tinsel, ornaments, and ribbons. The fresh blanket of snow muffling their footsteps lent the air a magical hush.

Without looking at him, Shelby could feel Travis's eyes on her.

Finally, the detective spoke, his warm breath frosting the air between them. "Shelby, can I ask ... did you really just get dizzy back there? It seemed like something more." When she didn't immediately respond, he continued gently. "You know you can tell me, right?"

She wrestled with herself. Could she trust him with the truth? Would he think she was crazy? But Travis had done nothing but treat her with respect and concern.

The detective said, "You seem to be able to sense

things others can't, and I think it's more than you just noticing things."

Shelby wasn't sure what he meant, but she was afraid to admit to having powers, thinking Travis would say she was nuts and he'd go away.

"Did you grow up in Hamlet?" she asked.

"No, I grew up in Salem. It's an interesting town," he told her. "There are lots of different kinds of people there. In fact, one of my friends is kind of a psychic. She can sense things about people and situations that turn out to be true. I've learned that keeping an open mind is the best thing to do." He watched Shelby's face.

"Oh?" Shelby said. "That's really interesting."

"I think so," Travis admitted.

Taking a deep breath, Shelby confessed. "All right ... when I touched that coin, I had some kind of ... vision." She went on to describe what she had seen, watching Travis closely for his reaction.

To her immense relief, he didn't recoil or express disbelief. Instead, he nodded thoughtfully. "I knew it," Travis said excitedly. "I had a sense you were picking up on things beyond the norm," he admitted. "You have abilities and sensitivities most others don't. Did you have some sort of psychic sensation when you looked at Mr. Peacock's coin collection?"

"Yes. I had a vision of someone going into Mr. Peacock's house. I could sense the person was dangerous and full of ill intent. I couldn't see the face though."

"Maybe if you hold one of the coins again, your vision will sharpen," Travis suggested.

"This paranormal stuff doesn't freak you out?" Shelby asked.

"Not one bit," Travis told her. "It's just another form beyond our five senses. Some people have extrasensory perception, and others don't. I think you're one of them. There are more things in this world than most people want to accept. I've seen enough in life not to reject something just because it's unfamiliar."

"That's a very mature way of looking at it." Shelby smiled at the detective.

"When Chief Martin of Sweet Cove told me I should collaborate with you, I knew exactly what he meant," Travis explained. "It's just hard to bring it up with someone."

A wide grin spread over Shelby's mouth as she shook her head. "It sure is hard. I expect people to shun me. I can't tell you how glad I am that you're so accepting. I really was afraid you'd run away screaming if I told you." She let out a sigh. "Though

I'll admit, some of what I can do now scares me a little. It just started recently after I hit my head. I'm still trying to understand it."

Travis nodded sympathetically. "That makes sense. Exploring talents like yours is uncharted territory, but if you ever want to talk about it, I'm here. I can't help with your new skills, but I can listen."

Impulsively, Shelby gave him a quick hug. "Thank you. You have no idea how much that means. I was so worried you'd think I was crazy or delusional if I told you."

"Never," Travis assured her sincerely. "I trust you, Shelby, and I'd like to help if I can." He chuckled. "Especially if your new skills can help us solve this case."

Shelby smiled up at him, feeling a swell of gratitude. "Actually, besides a couple of my friends, I haven't told a soul what's happening to me."

"Well, you told me, so that makes one more."

"Right." Shelby was so happy she could have skipped all the way home through the snow. "Thanks for not freaking out."

"I'm glad you told me. Would you be willing to hold one of the gold coins again to see if you have a clearer vision?"

"I'm so exhausted right now, I don't think it would be worthwhile." Shelby was sorry to disappoint the detective.

"I understand. Maybe another day? I can ask Mr. Peacock about it."

"Yeah, let's do it another time." Shelby was glad to try to have another vision because then she could see Travis again.

After seeing Shelby safely home, Travis headed to the station, his mind spinning. Learning about Shelby's burgeoning psychic talents gave him much to think about. He was determined to help her, as best he could, not just for the sake of the case, but for her own wellbeing.

He thought back to his old friend Claire in Salem who had psychic empath skills. She described it as being able to read people's energy and emotions. Travis had been skeptical at first, but over time, he came to trust in his friend's intuitive impressions as she unerringly zeroed in on things.

Clearly Shelby had profound sensitivity too, but of a different nature since she could apparently perceive events and details not visible to the eye. This could be Shelby's most valuable tool for cracking cases. Travis felt privileged she had confided in him. He hoped this marked a turning point of trust in their partnership, and maybe someday, something deeper between them.

Only time will tell.

21

It was late when Shelby sank back onto the plush sofa enjoying the warmth coming from the crackling fire in the bookshop. With Harper curled up beside her, she stretched her legs out on the ottoman and opened her laptop to do some paperwork for the shop.

Shelby made a few notes about inventory and upcoming events as snow squalls swirled past the frosted windows, and the old building settled with some creaks and groans.

Setting aside her work for a moment, Shelby reached over to stroke Harper's soft fur. "Thanks for being so understanding about me passing out at Mr. Peacock's house. I'm still trying to get a handle on these visions and senses. Having your support means a lot to me."

Harper lifted her head to meet the young woman's gaze. "Of course, I'm here anytime you want to talk through what you experienced. The more details you can give me, the more I may be able to help interpret it."

Shelby nodded slowly.

Harper asked, "Where did you say Mr. Peacock's coins were located?"

"The coins were displayed in a glass case in his study."

"Did a key open the case?" Harper asked.

"Yes, Mr. Peacock had a key," Shelby told the cat.

"How many coins were in the display box?"

"About ten. Why are you asking?" Shelby questioned the cat.

"Because Emily wants to know," Harper explains.

"Emily? The ghost?" Shelby sat up. "Why?"

"Because she wants to help Mr. Peacock." Harper shifted her eyes to a corner of the room and whispered, "But don't call her a ghost. She doesn't like the term."

"Okay," Shelby agreed. "This is wonderful that she wants to help. Is there anything else I can tell her?"

Emily's particles began to shimmer and swirl, and in a few seconds, the ghost materialized.

"Hello, Emily," Shelby told the transparent form.

The spirit floated a little above the floor and stared at Shelby for a few moments before quickly disappearing.

"Maybe I shouldn't have said anything to her," Shelby lamented.

"She wanted to show herself for a few seconds, but she didn't want to remain visible because it's too hard to speak to you," Harper explained.

"But why can she speak to you?" Shelby asked softly.

"Animals and spirits can communicate via the same wavelength. Speaking to humans takes up a lot of energy for a ghost so usually they avoid speaking to people," the cat explained.

"Wavelengths and energy? I don't know what that means, but I get the gist of it," Shelby admitted. "Does Emily know who wants to hurt Mr. Peacock?"

"She does not," Harper said.

Shelby nodded while letting out a sigh.

The cat twitched her tail thoughtfully. "When you touched one of the coins, you had a vivid vision. Can you describe again exactly what you saw?"

Shelby closed her eyes and went over the details

of the vision she'd had at Peacock's house. When she opened her eyes, Harper was staring intently at the corner of the room.

"Is Emily trying to tell us something?" Shelby asked excitedly.

"Yes, she wants to help protect Mr. Peacock if she can," explained the cat. After a thoughtful pause, Harper twitched her ears and reported, "Emily says the collections are important to solving the case."

"The coin collection or the art collection?" Shelby asked for clarification.

The cat nodded as she listened to Emily. "The coin collection."

"There must be a connection between those items and the motive, but what is it?" Shelby began pacing as she thought aloud, "Whoever killed that intruder was after something specific in Mr. Peacock's house. Were they targeting his collections?"

Harper suddenly went very still, fur bristling slightly along her back as she stared fixedly at the empty corner again.

"What is it, Harper?" Shelby asked worriedly. "What's happening?"

"Emily is feeling off. There's something going on that's disturbing the atoms in the air."

Shelby looked blank. "Translation?"

"Something isn't right," the cat explained.

"I know," Shelby said softly. "Someone was killed in Mr. Peacock's house and the killer is probably biding his time and will soon attack Mr. Peacock ... so Emily is correct, something isn't right at all."

Harper moved closer to the young woman. "Where's Lucy?"

"She went to a Christmas concert with Ross." Shelby became alarmed. "Is Lucy in danger? Is she hurt?"

"She's fine," Harper reports. "I asked about her because we could use more input and she always has something logical to contribute."

Shelby's eyes went wide. "Is the killer someone Mr. Peacock knows?"

"Emily isn't answering the question," the cat says. "Wait. Emily says, 'People often want what doesn't belong to them.'"

Shelby stood and clutched the rose quartz gem on her necklace. "The person who killed Emily wanted what wasn't his. Emily's stamp collection ... her killer murdered her to get at her stamp collection and gain access to her assets." Shivering, the skin on her arms prickled with unease. "Emily, if you know anything that could help, please give us guidance," she implored the hidden spirit.

After a long pause, Harper finally said, "Emily's message is that the person you know can be more dangerous than a stranger."

"So Mr. Peacock might actually be in danger from someone close to him?" Shelby asked sharply. "One of his friends maybe?"

"She can't elaborate further," said Harper apologetically. After another weighty silence, the cat added, "But Emily is repeating the phrase, 'People often want what is not theirs.'"

Pacing again, Shelby tapped her chin. "People want what's not theirs ... that must be key to the killer's motive here. Just like Emily's murderer - he killed her because he wanted her valuable stamp collection."

Stopping abruptly, Shelby swayed on her feet as the edges of her vision darkened, which indicated the now-familiar onset of a vision. She felt Harper trying to steady her as images began to flash before her mind's eye.

She saw a shadowy figure moving stealthily through a dark room. They seemed to be searching for something, growing increasingly agitated as they rifled through drawers and cabinets to no avail.

Finally, the person straightened, wheeled, and strode purposefully across the room. Reaching their target, they raised an object and brought it crashing down onto the head of the cowering man before them. The man collapsed to the floor.

With a ragged gasp, Shelby emerged from the vision touching Harper's fur to ground herself.

"Did you see something?" Harper asked intently.

Shelby nodded, still shaken by the violent vision. "The killer ..." She trailed off with a shudder. Trying to imprint the vision's details in her mind, she began to explain what she'd seen. Shelby wished Lucy were there to help analyze and make connections. She considered calling Travis to share what she had learned but a quick glance at the antique clock showed it was past midnight.

Too late for a call. Besides, the visions always left her drained and she wasn't sure she had the energy to explain what was going on.

Suddenly, a terrible wave of anxiety raced through the young woman's body. "Mr. Peacock."

"What is it?" Harper asked with concern.

Shelby leapt to her feet. "Mr. Peacock is in danger." She grabbed her phone and called Travis, but the detective didn't pick up so she left a message.

Next, she called Lucy, but the call went to voicemail so she left a message for her, too.

"Where is everyone when you need them?" Running to the closet, she grabbed her coat. "Come on, Harper. I'm having a premonition. We have to get out of here."

Shelby could feel it ... the clouded path was growing clearer.

22

Shelby crept through the snowy darkness surrounding James Peacock's house, with Harper pressed close at her heels. The property was still and silent except for a single light glowing from the back of the house. Unease skittered down Shelby's spine, her breaths coming out in frosty puffs in the freezing night air. She paused, pressing a gloved hand against the cold wall of the house to steady her nerves.

"Something's wrong here, Harper," she whispered, voicing her fears out loud. "I can feel it. I saw it in my mind. Mr. Peacock is in mortal danger." She swallowed hard and pressed her finger to her neck feeling her rose quartz gemstone beneath her heavy coat. "I'm afraid."

Harper gazed up at the young woman with luminous eyes that seemed to glow brighter in the darkness. "Trust your instincts, Shelby. Take a moment to center yourself, then listen to what they're telling you we should do next."

Shelby bit her bottom lip anxiously, glancing between the house and the street hoping for some sign of which path was right. Going in alone was dangerous and stupid, but waiting for Travis might cost them precious time. She wavered, uncertainty and dread twisting her insides.

Finally, after several agonizingly long moments, she turned back to her companion, new resolve steeling her spine. "You're right. I know what I need to do, but I'm still afraid."

"I'm right beside you," Harper told her.

Taking a deep, fortifying breath, she gave Harper a determined nod and moved silently through the snowy yard toward the back of the house. Shelby stuck close to the inky shadows encircling the place, relying on faint ambient light to pick her way cautiously in the darkness.

As she approached the back of Mr. Peacock's home, the indistinct sound of raised voices reached her ears. Shelby crept up the porch steps, her boots making barely a sound on the snow-dusted wood.

She held her breath as she slowly peered through the kitchen window.

Inside, the housekeeper Polly Sutter stood facing Mr. Peacock, in his pajamas and robe, gesturing aggressively as she shouted at the cowering man. His face was pale with fright and his eyes darted about as if looking for an escape route.

As she watched the ugly scene in the kitchen, fear and anger twisted in her gut.

Harper leapt into the young woman's arms so she could see what was going on inside the house. "That witch," Harper hissed to Shelby.

Just then, soft footsteps could be heard approaching from around the side of the house. Shelby whirled, her heart leaping into her throat, only to sag in relief as Lucy emerged into a pool of light from the porch lamp.

"Lucy." Shelby slipped quietly down the porch steps and hugged her friend. "How did you know I was back here?"

"Because there were boot prints and cat prints in the snow leading to the back of the house. I didn't think the killer brought a cat with him. What's going on?"

"Mr. Peacock is in danger. The housekeeper is inside yelling at him."

Lucy's voice trembled. "Is Polly the killer?"

"I think so. Mr. Peacock looks terrified."

Lucy's expression hardened with determination. "We have to get in there and help Mr. Peacock now," she whispered fiercely.

The two young women and the cat put their heads together and came up with a plan. Shelby steeled herself as they moved to the back door. Lucy stepped to the side with Harper and pressed her back against the outside wall of the house so as not to be seen. Shelby stood at the kitchen door pounding loudly on the solid wood.

"Mr. Peacock! It's Shelby, please open the door!"

No response came from within. Through the window she could see Polly glaring sharply at Peacock, one hand clamped on his arm preventing him from responding.

Exchanging a tense nod with Lucy, Shelby gathered herself. "Mr. Peacock. It's Shelby. I need your help. Please wake up." She kept pressing on the doorbell.

In frustration, Polly, with rage etched on her face, opened the door a crack. "It's after midnight," she snarled. "Mr. Peacock is ill. What are you doing here? What do you want?"

Lucy rushed forward like a linebacker, and she

and Shelby rammed the door open, throwing Polly off balance. Shelby gave the woman a push and she fell to the floor with a startled yelp.

"No, Shelby!" With his hands tied behind his back, Mr. Peacock shouted, "Get out. Run!"

But before they could react, heavy footsteps pounded down the hall as a powerfully-built man appeared brandishing a pistol.

"Don't move!" he barked menacingly.

Fear raced through Shelby at the sight of the intruder and his weapon. Polly scrambled to her feet and pushed the two women into kitchen chairs at the man's gruff direction. Clearly, this was her accomplice.

Dread settled like a rock in Shelby's stomach. "Who are you?" she demanded.

Polly snarled, "He's my husband, Don. Too bad you're such a nosy pain in the butt."

Keeping the gun trained on the young women, the man began interrogating Peacock about his coin collection, spittle flying as he raged. "Where are those coins? Tell me where they are, old man, or you all die tonight."

"Don't tell him, Mr. Peacock," Shelby said with determination. "The coins belong to you."

"Shut up," Don yelled as he stormed toward the

young woman. He cracked the heavy pistol across Shelby's face in uncontrolled fury.

Pain exploded through her head from the blow and she could taste blood in her mouth. *Don't pass out, don't pass out.*

As she struggled to remain alert, she glimpsed Harper slinking stealthily along the floor behind Don, fixing Shelby with an intense stare. Their eyes locked, and an understanding passed between them. Shelby gave an almost imperceptible nod.

"I'll tell you where the coins are," Mr. Peacock shouted.

"Don't tell him." Shelby spit a bit of blood onto the floor as Lucy moved a little closer to Peacock. "Don't tell him where the coins are, Mr. Peacock. These people think they can take whatever they want. They can't. Not tonight. Not ever."

Polly looked at Shelby as if she were suddenly afraid of her, and that's when Shelby felt a surge of power flood through her veins. Making eye contact with Lucy, she mustered her courage and cried, "Now!"

Chaos erupted.

Lucy stood and tackled Peacock to the ground, shielding his body with her own. Harper flew across the room and leapt forward sinking her claws into

Don's calf before scrambling up to claw at his face with a fierce yowl. At the same moment, Shelby crashed into his legs with all her strength, toppling the large man.

The gun flew from Don's grip, skidding across the tile floor and under the table. Shelby lunged for it, her hands shaking violently with adrenaline and terror as she tried to reach for the cold metal.

Harper slid the weapon closer until Shelby could grab it.

Using two hands, she held the gun out in front of her, alternating pointing it at Don and Polly.

"Who are you?" Polly whispered backing away from Shelby.

"Police! Freeze! Down on the ground!" Detective Whitely rushed into the kitchen with his gun drawn, and his jaw dropped when he saw Don lying on the ground, Peacock and Lucy on the floor, Harper padding over to him, and Shelby holding a weapon.

Shelby nearly sobbed in relief at the sight of him and the other officers. It was over now. Travis quickly took control of the scene with calm authority, handcuffing a cursing Don and Polly.

"They were threatening Mr. Peacock for his coin collection. They threatened to kill us, but we're all okay." Shelby walked over to him and handed him the gun. "I don't even know how to shoot it."

Travis let out a long breath, smiled, and squeezed Shelby's arm.

While Lucy helped Mr. Peacock to his feet, Shelby rushed over and threw her arms around them both. "Thank goodness you're okay," she cried, emotion cracking her voice. The adrenaline still fizzing through her system made her limbs tremble.

"Our plan worked." Lucy beamed.

"I don't know what I would have done if anything happened to you," Shelby told her friend.

"Well, nothing did," Lucy said with a smile. "We're safe and sound."

Mr. Peacock shook his head in disbelief. "You saved my life. All three of you," he said earnestly, meeting each of their eyes in turn. He leaned down to scruff Harper's neck affectionately as she purred and rubbed against him. "I cannot thank you enough."

The man touched his forehead. "They told me they killed that poor man who was in my house while I was at the conference. They told me they were going to kill me, too, once they got the coin collection." Mr. Peacock swayed on his feet.

An ambulance pulled up to the curb with emergency lights painting the snow red and blue, and EMTs rushed into the house.

"Let's get you and Mr. Peacock looked at," Travis said gently.

The adrenaline draining away, Shelby listed to one side when an EMT approached her, the pain from her injuries finally registering along with bone-deep exhaustion.

After being tended to by the medical professionals, Shelby sat gratefully sipping hot coffee, the warmth seeping through her as the harrowing events replayed in her mind. She recounted everything in minute detail to Travis as he listened attentively.

The detective sat beside the young woman studying her solemnly, his shoulder just brushing hers. "What you and Lucy did in here was incredibly brave confronting the criminals like that. It was also a very reckless thing to do. You're lucky to be alive, but your actions saved Mr. Peacock's life."

Shelby managed a shaky smile, wincing as the motion pulled at her swollen cheek and split lip. "I didn't have a choice. It was that or let them kill Mr. Peacock. When I got here and saw Polly threatening him, I couldn't wait for backup." She shook her head ruefully. "Not the wisest choice I've ever made, but I did what I had to do in the moment."

Travis nodded. "I understand, and you did exactly the right thing under the circumstances." He gently grasped her shoulder, his expression grave. "But please, Shelby, promise me you won't take a risk like that again. Please."

"I promise, I'll try," Shelby assured him sincerely, unexpectedly warmed by his protectiveness. She knew he was right - she had gotten lucky.

When it was Lucy's turn to give her statement, Shelby ushered Mr. Peacock to the living room sofa, and when they sat down, Harper jumped on the man's lap and snuggled with him.

"It's been a long, long night," Shelby said. "After all the excitement, I'm feeling sort of weak."

Mr. Peacock patted her hand. "Then we shall take care of each other, my dear friend."

Harper threw back her head and let out a long, happy howl.

23

Shelby and Lucy were finally allowed to head home as the sky lightened with dawn's first rosy fingers. Shelby's face ached and she was so fatigued she could barely shuffle up to her apartment. With Harper settling beside her, she had never been more grateful to crawl under the soft blankets and sheets that felt like heaven, sinking immediately into a deep and dreamless slumber.

Over the next week, life slowly returned to its familiar rhythms. Don and Polly Sutter quickly confessed everything under questioning. They had conspired together to rob and kill Mr. Peacock after Polly learned about his valuable coin collection from her housekeeping work for him. In a rage fueled by greed and cruelty, Don had viciously murdered the unsuspecting intruder Allen Jones when he found him in the house and mistook him for Mr. Peacock. Don was employed as a custodian at the Harris Estate and when he realized he'd murdered the wrong man, he knew he had to get rid of the body before the real Mr. Peacock came home. He snuck the body into the mansion through a side door and dumped him in one of the sitting rooms before setting the dead man on fire.

With the case finally solved and the culprits soon to be behind bars where they belonged, it felt as if a huge oppressive weight had lifted from Shelby's shoulders. She spent long cozy evenings with Lucy rehashing everything that had happened as they celebrated the successful conclusion to the case, and the Spellbound Bookshop bustled with holiday shoppers keeping Shelby happily busy.

One snowy night, Shelby entered the cozy bookshop after closing to finish up some gift wrapping behind the counter. A familiar prickling sensation on the back of her neck made her turn. Emily's ghostly outline hovered transparently beside the front window, silver moonlight streaming through her misty form.

A wide smile broke across Shelby's face. She inclined her head respectfully toward the apparition. "Emily ... I hope you can understand me. I wanted to thank you for your warning the other night. Mr. Peacock is happy and well, and his coin collection is safe from the thieves."

The spirit drifted closer, a small smile showing on her face. Slowly, she extended a hand, the wispy fingers stopping just short of touching Shelby's cheek.

Shelby felt the faintest whisper-soft caress of energy against her skin. "You're welcome," Emily's faint voice echoed gently inside her mind.

And then the ghost silently faded away like mist under the warmth of the morning sun. Shelby's eyes shone with grateful tears. Even from beyond the veil between life and death, Emily had reached out to protect a citizen of the town that had been hers so long ago.

A familiar sound of the treats jar rattling drew Shelby's attention. Turning, she saw Harper eagerly pawing at the lid, fixing her with an insistent stare.

With a laugh, Shelby obligingly opened the jar and tipped some salmon-flavored treats onto the counter in front of the cat. Stroking Harper's back gently, she murmured, "You're welcome too, Harper. And thank you for helping me, my friend. We make a pretty great team, don't we?"

Harper chirped her emphatic agreement before happily crunching the treats. Together, the two of them, along with Lucy and Travis had faced darkness and had successfully emerged from it with their perseverance, courage, and friendship.

A few nights before Christmas, Shelby bustled around her cozy apartment putting the final touches on the decorations and food for the Christmas party. A fresh fir garland wrapped in warm white lights adorned the fireplace mantel, filling the space with the lovely scent of pine. The mouthwatering aromas of chicken parmesan, yeasty rolls, and gingerbread cookies fresh from the oven drifted through the room.

Right on time, the cheery sound of the doorbell rang out and Harper trotted over to see who it was while Shelby opened the door to see Lucy and Ross bearing dishes heaped with appetizers and sides to add to the feast.

"Come on in. Let me take those off your hands," Shelby welcomed them warmly, relieving them of the heavy platters.

Soon more guests filtered in as the apartment

and the space began to buzz with happy voices - Shelby's parents John and Ginny, her brother Adam and his girlfriend Lauren, Julie Hill and Mr. Peacock who looked distinguished in his suit jacket, Patrice and her husband Ron, Fiona the psychic and her rugged husband Tyler, Rachel from the bookstore accompanied by her boyfriend Chad the barista, and finally Detective Whitely arrived straight from work looking sharp in a suit and tie.

The space was packed and it was soon filled with warmth and lively conversation. Shelby's holiday playlist jingled in the background as people mingled and snacked, while Harper weaved among their ankles hopefully angling for dropped appetizers and affectionate pats. Soon, they broke into smaller groups to play board games and cards.

When dinner was ready, the cheerful group crowded around the long table, elbow to elbow, and passed platters and bowls to each other family-style. Shelby gazed fondly around at the smiling, familiar faces. Friends both old and new, they had all become part of her extended family.

Catching Travis's eye from across the table, they shared a smile that brought color rising in Shelby's cheeks. She offered silent words of thanks for every person under her roof.

Over apple pie, cookies, and coffee, the talk turned to the dramatic and near-tragic event surrounding the case just a week prior.

"I can hardly believe what you went through that night, Shel." Her brother Adam shook his head in awe. "Those two thieves were mighty bold to commit murder over some coins."

Lucy nodded solemnly, her blonde hair shining in the firelight. "Desperation drives people to commit terrible deeds, but taking a life is never justified, no matter how dire someone's circumstances."

"What confuses me is, how much could a private coin collection really be worth?" mused Ginny with a puzzled frown. "A few thousand dollars at the very most, I'd think."

"Far more than you might assume," Peacock responded mildly. "I actually had the full collection appraised by an expert recently. I believe Polly heard me on the phone one day when I was speaking with the appraiser. I've owned the Queen Elizabeth II Canadian Gold Maple Leaf coins for some time and thought I should update the insurance on them. I was quite floored when the appraiser told me they were worth over three hundred and fifty thousand dollars."

A stunned silence met the news, quickly

followed by exclamations of disbelief around the table.

"Did I hear that correctly?" Fiona's husband Tyler asked, one eyebrow cocked in surprise. "Those old coins turned out to be quite the shrewd investment."

Mr. Peacock looked faintly amused by the attention, but he nodded in confirmation. "Antique coins can be remarkably valuable. I confess I had no notion of their true worth when I first began collecting them years ago as a hobby, but some quite rare treasures ended up in my collection over time."

Mr. Peacock sipped from his coffee mug. "Looking back, I believe Polly overheard what the collection was worth, and then she and her husband set a plan in motion to steal the coins."

"Well, now the desperation of those crooks makes perfect sense," Adam remarked grimly. A somber mood fell over the group as the implications of this sank in. Shelby reached out to give Peacock's hand a comforting squeeze.

Seeking to revive the cheery atmosphere, Shelby's mother spoke up into the lull. "This evening should be filled with the spirit of the season, not darkened by grim thoughts or deeds," she gently admonished.

Turning a questioning look on Shelby, Ginny continued, "What I am curious about is, what made you go over to check on Mr. Peacock that night in the first place, dear? Did you suspect something specific was amiss?"

Shelby considered the question, cradling the warm mug of spiced cider in her hands. "You know, looking back I'm not totally sure what came over me," she finally said. "I just had this sudden overpowering sense of foreboding, an urgent feeling that Mr. Peacock was in terrible danger."

She shook her head ruefully. "It was like I was compelled to go to him right that instant. I didn't even think to call him first or wait for backup - I just reacted on pure instinct."

"She's always had good instincts and intuition," John remarked approvingly over his glasses, pride for his daughter evident in his crinkled smile.

"It was her intuition guiding her," Fiona proclaimed, nodding sagely. "We all receive promptings at times from our subconscious mind that we can't logically comprehend, but they come for an important reason. Sometimes, we have a feeling that we don't understand. We often don't listen to it. Modern life has downplayed the importance of listening to our intuition. We all need to remember to listen to what our minds are telling us. How many times have we heard about someone feeling that something was off? I've read about young women who were approached by a criminal and they sensed something was wrong and were able to get away because they listened to their feelings."

Nodding slowly as she considered this perspective, Shelby said, "You make an excellent point, Fiona. At the time it was this strange innate sense of impending trouble that I didn't stop to analyze." She met her mentor's knowing gaze. "You're right about how important it is to listen to those subtle intuitive nudges instead of dismissing anything we can't readily explain."

"Regardless of the source, the urgent impression that prompted Shelby into action undoubtedly saved my life that night," Mr. Peacock remarked solemnly. "There are many mysteries in this world, but clearly trusting your instincts can prove vitally important."

Murmurs of wholehearted agreement sounded around the table. Shelby smiled gratefully at their acknowledgements. Though her developing intuitive powers still mystified her much of the time, she was gradually learning to trust in their subtle guidance without putting up resistance.

As the hour grew late, the party wound down

reluctantly with profuse thanks given and accepted for Shelby's role in keeping Mr. Peacock from harm. Promises were made to meet again soon in the new year for more good food and fellowship.

Soon the only guest remaining was Travis who insisted on staying behind to help clean up. Working in tandem, they quickly restored order to the apartment's kitchen and living room.

With everything clean and put away, they sank onto the sofa beside the softly glowing fireplace. Harper immediately hopped up onto Shelby's lap and settled in, kneading contentedly as Shelby gently stroked her fur.

She turned to face Travis, the flickering firelight playing over his handsome features. "I'm so glad you came tonight," she said softly.

Travis's dark eyes were tender as he gazed back at her. "I wouldn't have missed it for the world. After everything that's happened recently, it was really good to see you happy and relaxed."

He hesitated, then continued in a low voice. "I'm happy to be counted as one of your friends."

Shelby's breath caught at the vulnerability she heard in his words. "You definitely are," she whispered.

Electricity arced between them, but neither one was ready to make the first move.

Wanting to break the tension between them, Shelby smiled and asked, "Want to watch a Christmas movie?"

Travis chuckled. "Yeah, I do, but is there a Christmas movie that has a crime in it?"

Shaking her head, Shelby asked, "Don't you get enough of crime in your daily life?"

Travis shrugged. "I like crime shows."

As the fire cast its warm, rosy glow over the room, snow flurries swirled past the frosted windows. With a purring Harper resting on her lap and Travis sitting next to her, Shelby let out a deep, contented sigh. She unconsciously reached for the gemstone on her necklace and rubbed it between her thumb and index finger. She couldn't have imagined a better ending to the tumultuous events of the past weeks.

The holidays could be a magical season and Shelby knew she had been blessed with the best gifts of all - family, her bookstore, Lucy, Harper, her friends, and a few newfound talents. It was more than she'd ever dared to dream.

Out of the corner of her eye, she took a quick

peek at Travis, and a rush of warmth spread through her.

She couldn't wait to see what would happen next.

I hope you enjoyed *Pages and Premonitions*! The next book in the series, *Secrets and Psychics*, can be found here:

https://mybook.to/SecretsandPsychics

THANK YOU FOR READING!

Books by J.A. WHITING can be found here:
amazon.com/author/jawhiting

To hear about new books and book sales, please sign up for my mailing list at:
jawhiting.com

Your email will never be sold, shared, or spammed.

If you enjoyed the book, please consider leaving a review. A few words are all that's needed. It would be very much appreciated.

BOOKS BY J. A. WHITING

SPELLBOUND BOOKSHOP PARANORMAL COZY MYSTERIES

SWEET COVE PARANORMAL COZY MYSTERIES

LIN COFFIN PARANORMAL COZY MYSTERIES

CLAIRE ROLLINS PARANORMAL COZY MYSTERIES

MURDER POSSE PARANORMAL COZY MYSTERIES

PAXTON PARK PARANORMAL COZY MYSTERIES

ELLA DANIELS WITCH COZY MYSTERIES

SEEING COLORS PARANORMAL COZY MYSTERIES

OLIVIA MILLER MYSTERIES (not cozy)

SWEET ROMANCES by JENA WINTER

COZY BOX SETS

BOOKS BY J.A. WHITING & NELL MCCARTHY

HOPE HERRING PARANORMAL COZY MYSTERIES

TIPPERARY CARRIAGE COMPANY COZY MYSTERIES

BOOKS BY J.A. WHITING & ARIEL SLICK

GOOD HARBOR WITCHES PARANORMAL COZY MYSTERIES

BOOKS BY J.A. WHITING & AMANDA DIAMOND

PEACHTREE POINT COZY MYSTERIES

DIGGING UP SECRETS PARANORMAL COZY MYSTERIES

BOOKS BY J.A. WHITING & MAY STENMARK

MAGICAL SLEUTH PARANORMAL WOMEN'S FICTION COZY MYSTERIES

HALF MOON PARANORMAL MYSTERIES

VISIT US

jawhiting.com

bookbub.com/authors/j-a-whiting

amazon.com/author/jawhiting

facebook.com/jawhitingauthor

bingebooks.com/author/ja-whiting

Made in United States
Orlando, FL
07 February 2024

43418190R00178